REBECCA STEELE
FINDING THE DREAM
BOOK 2

JOANNE PATTERSON

ISBN: 978-0-578-68481-9
Printed in the United States of America

In memory of Jane McCabe,
who instilled in me the love of horses.

MESSAGE FROM THE AUTHOR

Some of you have been with Becky before and some are just meeting her for the first time. I promised those of you who've read the first book she'd be back.

I want to thank all of you for being here with us. Becky has become a part of me through this writing process and I appreciate so much that many of you have become attached to her too. Emily is back as her best friend along with some others that you will recognize and new characters that I hope you come to love.
I promise you following Becky will be fun and interesting. She is the same sincere loving character that she was in the first book just a little smarter and wiser. She rides horses now instead of traveling on airplanes.

Please leave any comments you may have on my author page:
www.facebook.com/authorjoannepatterson

Enjoy Becky's adventures as she continues her music career and makes a splash in the world of rodeos and cowboys in Nashville. I hope y'all enjoy reading as much as I enjoyed writing. I wish you the very best always.

Joanne

ACKNOWLEDGEMENTS

To Kate, my dear friend and excellent editor who honestly gives me her opinion, encourages me to write, won't let me quit and has taught me so much. Also to Julie, my "Emily" who listens to storylines and ideas at all hours and keeps telling me I really do know how to write.

Introduction/Prologue

NASHVILLE TENNESSEE

When I was a little girl I would spend most of my day outside playing with the neighbor's puppies, feeding the squirrels or giving sugar to the horses people rode down my street. I loved animals and because I was an only child these creatures became my family. My dad worked long hours as a stockbroker and my mom was busy taking care of our house while working part-time as a seamstress. I learned to be happy doing things by myself. Once I started school, I had friends around me but still preferred spending time with animals. I was not allowed to have a cat or dog of my own so I adopted everyone else's. I daydreamed a lot, imagining myself all grown up and living in a big house with animals everywhere. Sometimes our biggest dreams are based on experience and some are glimpses of our destiny yet to be fulfilled.

What is destiny? Like many things, life and love got in the way and seemed to take me off course. It took me from a career in the airlines to stardom in Nashville. It brought a friendship with my friend Emily who would become the best friend ever. It saw me through an early marriage, which ended in divorce. It ultimately brought me to the air show circuit where I would come to meet Johnny who would change the way I looked at love. My longing, loving and losing made me more cautious and when all was said and done I learned he could not prioritize me. I got involved with his best friend Mike. All the while my singing career moved forward and my priorities were continually shifting.

"Nice moves, Becky," I said to myself, "You've just dodged two bullets."

An engagement was broken, a ring returned and a love affair laid to rest after being dead for 20 years. It became obvious to me as Mike and I spent more time together that he was not my destiny. The relationship was nothing more than a glorified rebound after Johnny.

I had to be honest with him and a short time after a beach incident on Hilton Head Island we agreed marriage was not in the cards for us. Hoping for new beginnings and better endings, Mike begrudgingly went back to Charlotte to live with his sons and I happily went back to my apartment in Nashville.

Johnny unwillingly went back to his life in Perry, Georgia. No matter what I said or how I said it, he refused to believe there was nothing left between us. He told me he would never give up. Little did I know that after living for him for so long I could eventually have the freedom to move forward and make my own dreams come true. I was determined to become a SUPERSTAR.

Chapter 1
NASHVILLE TENNESSEE

My friend Emily's retirement party was in full swing and she was enjoying every moment. The music was LOUD. You could hear the bass in the parking lot of The Hummingbird Café. I watched from the background as airline friends congratulated her and wished her the best of luck. Twenty years is a long time. Now that we were both retired, we wondered what our next adventure would be. Well, stay tuned, we were about to find out.

Marty, the owner of The Hummingbird, motioned for me to sit with him at a table. He was not only my manager, he had become like a father to me since my parents were killed in a car accident on highway 65 outside Nashville a few years back. He was good looking for a man in his late fifties and had plenty of white hair, which was smashed down from wearing a cowboy hat. He had heard through the grapevine the apartment building where Emily and I lived was being sold to a developer for a shopping center. He asked Emily to join us for some conversation about this.

The band took a break for a few minutes so it was quiet enough to talk. Marty wanted to ask us something. He needed some help with his quarter horse ranch in nearby Franklin since his two sons had gone off to college.

1

The ranch was located on a huge compound consisting of the main house in the center where Marty and his wife Dixie lived, a modern bunkhouse where the cowboys stayed and a brand new rustic building for the ten or so guests who came for a fun dude ranch experience every week. This building had a huge dining room, a fireplace and a wraparound porch with views of the ranch from all angles. Plenty of outdoor furniture dotted the porch. A huge brick outdoor gas pizza oven was built into the wall by the sliding glass doors.

The stables were away from the houses near acres of pasture. They were painted a happy red and the houses were painted a pristine white with red trim. A modern white split rail fence surrounded the pastures. A little ways down a dirt road a smaller three-bedroom ranch was nestled in the trees. This white house had been vacant since Marty's sons grew up and left home.

A huge custom-made sign with a bay quarter horse stallion sat at the edge of the property welcoming visitors to THE HUMMINGBIRD QUARTER HORSE RANCH. Colorful shasta daisies were planted as far as the eye could see. What a lovely setting for one of the largest ranches in Tennessee!

Marty asked Emily what she wanted to do with her life since she had just retired. He already knew I had my music career. Emily however, was clueless about her future. Marty then asked both of us if we would like to live in the three bedroom home on the ranch and help him run the business. The Hummingbird Café, which he had owned for many years was taking up all of his time. There were songwriters and musicians who made it their second home and he was very busy working with them. He then asked Emily if she could cook. I was glad he didn't ask me. He assured me I could bring my three horses and my shelties to live on the ranch. Emily and I looked at each other. Within about a minute we both said, "Yes!" in unison. A big smile stole across Marty's face.

A dream I'd had since I was a child was coming true. I could see the smiles on my parents' faces in heaven. They always knew how much this would mean to me.

The details would have to be worked out but for now Emily would run the restaurant division of the dude ranch operation and I would take the guests on trail rides and do whatever was necessary for them to enjoy their stay. I would work with the horses whenever there was time. We high-fived each other and hugged Marty for this great opportunity. He was beyond relieved to have two of his favorite people living on the ranch and helping him out. There were also other employees on the ranch including a full-time cook and a groundskeeper who worked very hard keeping the landscaping looking beautiful. In addition there was a housekeeping staff on duty 24 hours a day, kept busy by the huge turnover in guests at the dude ranch. Volunteers who just wanted to be around the horses helped out doing odd chores. It was a happy bunch.

Chapter 2
FRANKLIN TENNESSEE

Emily poured me a welcome cup of hot coffee. It was fun to be living together. There was plenty of room in this three-bedroom ranch house. She only had a few minutes before guests would be coming into the dining room of the dude ranch for breakfast. Emily had the sole responsibility for running this part of the ranch and she did a darned good job. People enjoyed the complimentary breakfast and the trail rides that were scheduled soon after. The dude ranch was very popular among the tourists who visited this part of Tennessee.

"Hey Becky," Emily said, "I see the application for Miss Rodeo Tennessee is still sitting on the counter. You've only filled out the first line with your name. Why haven't you filled out the rest of it and sent it in?"

I took a sip of coffee and explained that I wasn't sure I wanted to vie for the title. There were a lot of applicants.

Emily answered, "So what? You've got them all beat by a mile." I thanked my lifelong best friend for her confidence and told her I'd think very seriously about it.

"You'd better hurry up," Emily said as she finished her coffee. "There's only one more week until the deadline." We gave each other a hug as she left.

"I'll tell you my decision later, Emily, after I finish the trail rides. I always think about things when I'm riding Skipper."

When I returned from a long trail ride in the great outdoors, I had decided to throw my hat into the ring for Miss Rodeo Tennessee.

There were two weeks until the rodeo competition, which started with an apparel and public speaking entry and finished with a horsemanship entry the following day. The two non-riding events were held at the Western Saloon. There was also a private ten-minute interview backstage with the panel of judges, which included the current Miss Rodeo Tennessee, a country music star and two previous rodeo competitors. The winner would be crowned at the rodeo in Franklin. I had to admit I'd always wanted the silver and gold buckle awarded as first prize. Luckily I had some experience barrel racing and Skipper had been trained for this event.

Marty told me I had been chosen to lead the procession into the rodeo arena. What an honor!

My western wardrobe needed some help. My good friend Julie shopped for me when I needed new clothes. She found me some new duds for the apparel competition. As she held up a new shirt I couldn't help but notice her strawberry blonde hair and blue eyes. She looked like a movie star.

"I've got my boots and hat." I told her. "Just find a sharp outfit in a pretty color, like turquoise. I don't need to wear chaps."

She answered, "I'm on it!" and was off in a flash. She was such a good friend and kept me on track when my life got hectic.

Now that I was officially a contestant, I had to decide what I wanted to talk about for the public speaking event. I chose country music. No surprise there. I received an email welcoming me to the competition and informing me Martina McBride would be one of the judges! She was one of my favorites and lived nearby in Nashville.

There was so much to do! I used Emily as a sounding board for my talk and I felt confident it was informative and entertaining. The outfit Julie found was a pretty turquoise color and had gold trim on the blouse and cuffs. The interview could be about anything so I would just have to wing it. Skipper and I were ready for the riding competition.

The competitions went off without a hitch. I had to admit there were some beautiful young women trying out. I was nervous before the interview but I took some deep breaths and answered honestly without hesitation.

Skipper and I excelled at the riding competition as he flew around the barrels, performing exactly as he was trained to do. What a great competitor he was!

Chapter 3
FOUR YEARS EARLIER

Adam Mason, a State Police officer from Upstate New York, had just relocated to Franklin, Tennessee with his mother and father. The warm weather would be a welcome change from the brutal winters in New York. His interest in rodeos brought him to this western town near Nashville, where there were huge horse ranches interspersed with expensive homes.

Adam was busy making new friends on the rodeo circuit. Dillon, a bronc rider from Wyoming, sat next to him one day in the local coffee shop. Adam was explaining he had a nickname, "Chance," which had stuck with him since he was a kid. He was always trying different things and would take a chance on anything.

Dillon said, "Okay, Chance it is," and they shook hands.

At the same time two attractive women arrived and sat at the nearby counter. One of them, an attractive blonde with long hair, caught Chance's eye.

Do you know the pretty blonde at the counter? " he asked Dillon.

Dillon smiled and replied, "Get in line buddy. Her family owns a big quarter horse ranch near here and they also own The Hummingbird Café in Nashville."

Chance told his new friend that he would have to remember her.

"By the way, what's her name?" he asked.

Dillon replied, "Becky, her name is Becky Steele."

Chapter 4

What a glorious sunny day for the Franklin, Tennessee rodeo! There were flowers everywhere, around the edges of the arena and along the procession route. All the children were given small American flags to wave.

The crowd cheered wildly as I proudly carried the American flag for the first time and led the procession into the rodeo arena. I was wearing my white signature cowboy hat and my favorite red cowboy boots. Skipper, my five-year old sorrel quarter horse gelding moved along gracefully, oblivious to the noise of all the fans in the stands. Skipper and I were a team. The announcer explained the workings of each event as it took place so everyone easily understood what was going on.

First up were the bronc and bull riding events. The crowd cheered as cowboy after cowboy bit the dust. Next, the timed events were front and center. The calf roping, steer wrestling and crowd-favorite barrel racers brought the fans to their feet. The two trick buffaloes were last to perform with Chance, a trick rodeo performer, working his magic much to the delight of the crowd. He actually stood on the back of his horse and did all his rope tricks! It was pretty impressive. All the girls loved Chance. However, it was obvious to everyone he was fond of me and tipped his hat as he rode by.

After the events, there was a call for the Miss Rodeo Tennessee competitors to line up in a row inside the arena. Next there was a short speech thanking all for entering and explaining how difficult the final decision had been. The competition was based on points, with the highest total determining the winner. I was so nervous I thought I was going to be sick. Skipper felt my nerves and started pawing the ground.

Finally the speech was over and the top administrator of the Tennessee Rodeo Association walked out with the famous gold and silver buckle in his hand. He walked down the line shaking everyone's hand, thanking them for competing.

"Will you please hurry up," I was thinking to myself, as I felt faint.

He stood in front of the contestants and as the packed arena became silent, the announcer called out, "The winner of this year's Miss Rodeo Tennessee is…MISS BECKY STEELE!"

He walked over to Skipper's side, shook my hand and handed me the buckle. He then placed the gold tiara on my white hat. I thought I was dreaming. The crowd was clapping and cheering. One by one, the other contestants rode over and shook my hand and congratulated me. My heart was beating out of my chest. Emily walked next to me smiling.

"See, Becky, I told you you'd win."

I was over the moon with excitement. I really never expected to win. I thought of my momma and how proud she would be. I hoped she was watching from heaven.

When everything had calmed down and most of the spectators had left, I rode Skipper over to the holding area where I dismounted, uncinched his saddle and gave him some hay to munch on. I hugged his neck and told him what a good boy he was and how proud I was of him. He was the first foal from my bay mare, Misty. People were still coming over and congratulating me. It was very exciting and humbling at the same time.

BAAM! All of a sudden out of nowhere one of the wild buffaloes came tearing around the corner with Chance holding a broken lead in his hand. Skipper reared and knocked me over. I remember trying to hold on to him and then hurting my arm as I hit the ground. I could hear the siren of an ambulance far away in my head. There is always an ambulance on standby on a rodeo site and the paramedics were at my side in a flash.

When I opened my eyes the next morning, Emily was in the hospital with me. I asked her where I was. She filled me in on what happened. Apparently I hit my head on a rock when I fell and sprained my arm. One of the wranglers had grabbed Skipper and screamed for an ambulance. She took a minute and called Marty and Dixie, who were in Nashville working at their Hummingbird Café. They rushed to the hospital but there was nothing they could do. The fact that I won the title was lost in everyone's concern about my welfare. Dixie, a very attractive woman with blonde tipped hair, came into the room to tell me that the doctors said as far as they could tell there were no major brain injuries. Hopefully I would be able to go home in a few hours. She said that Emily had spent the night in a chair next to my bed. She had even put her headphones on me hoping the country music would wake me up. I asked about Skipper and wanted to be sure he was calm and taken care of. He must have been terrified to rear up like that. Emily reassured me that he was fine at home in the pasture chilling out.

The nurses limited visitors to two at a time but it seemed unnecessary as I was recovering quickly. I was so glad to see my friends; I couldn't stop crying. I told Emily to go home and get some sleep.

"Just check on my dogs, will you? They won't understand why I'm not there."

Emily hugged me and said she'd make sure my dogs were taken care of too.

Chapter 5

The doctor finally arrived and told me they had to do more tests. It looked like I had some amnesia related to the fall. He wanted Emily to be in the room when he asked me about my life.

There seemed like a million questions. He started with long-term experiences when I was in my twenties. He progressed up through the years until the present. This all took a couple of hours. My answers indicated very little short-term loss but there were significant issues into my twenties and thirties. He told us not to be too concerned because usually the memories come back after a short time. He wanted Emily to show me pictures of my past and keep track of what I remembered.

I was not allowed to ride horseback or do any heavy work for a couple of weeks. He told me to make an appointment for a two-week follow up.

"You were very lucky," he told me. "This could have had an entirely different outcome." Even though the memory of events when I was younger was very sporadic, he didn't seem too concerned. Dixie asked me if I remembered anything while I was unconscious.

"I don't really know, " I replied. "I had some pretty wild colorful dreams but don't remember anything specific other than a lot of country music and an airplane or two."

Chance arrived and stood in the hallway until I motioned for him to come in. He was beyond sorry about what happened because he was feeling responsible. He explained the rope split in two, allowing the buffalo to run free.

"Thank goodness you're not badly hurt," he said to me. "I don't know what I'd do if you were." I gently took his hand and assured him it was just a terrible accident and I was going to be as good as new very soon. I liked Chance but we were more friends than anything else.

With the doctor's release, Marty and Dixie gathered me up and brought me home to our Hummingbird Quarter Horse Ranch. I cried with relief when I saw my horses and my dogs. They meant everything to me.

They wanted me to stay at the main house for a few days. Emily came over from the dude ranch to give me a big hug. There was even a huge banner draped across the front of the main house, which read: MISS RODEO TENNESSEE LIVES HERE. CONGRATULATIONS BECKY!

I was so happy to be home.

Chapter 6

There were more memory tests to come. Emily found a scrapbook and asked me questions about the pictures. I remembered my parents, Rodney and Martha Steele, but I didn't remember that they had been killed in a car accident on highway 65. I never drove on this highway and always wondered why. I cried for hours as if it had just happened. I remembered some of the people I worked with at the airport but had trouble with their names. When Emily asked me whether I remembered the Silver Eagles or traveling to the air shows, I had no idea even though she said this was a huge part of my life.

As we got closer to the present, things improved. With Emily's help, I started to remember Hilton Head Island and the Beach Club. I sort of remembered the house Emily and I stayed in when we were on vacation. I still have dreams of how beautiful the ocean was.

The doctor was encouraged and said the memories would probably come back in bits and pieces and I should write everything down so as to not forget what I had remembered.

Chapter 7

I picked up my scrapbooks to try to jog my memory. I saw in my mother's handwriting something I said when I was a child. As soon as I could talk I would say to anyone who would listen, "Horse like Trigger, dog like Lassie." My parents could never figure out how I knew about these fictional animals. Throughout my life I would indeed come to have a horse that looked like Trigger and many shelties that looked like Lassie.

A week or so later, things were getting pretty much back to normal except for my memory. Marty and I were discussing whether I was well enough to go out on a trail ride. I was sure that I was okay even though he wasn't convinced.

"I can take the guests on a trail ride! I'll take it easy and not do anything stupid."

Marty reluctantly agreed. We had a full-time wrangler, Ryan, who was advised not to let me lift anything. I really got along well with him and he was more than happy to make sure I was taken care of. Ryan was the typical lanky cowboy with rugged good looks and twinkling blue eyes.

Over at the dude ranch Emily was going crazy as the food order had not arrived on time. She had the full responsibility for the operation and it seemed like something was always going wrong.

She had to send one of the waitresses into town to purchase what she needed.

The guests loved the wrap-around porch where breakfast was served. There was a hammock and a swing set along with many chairs and tables. From the porch, guests could see a full view of the ranch and all the horses out to pasture.

My three horses were in a pasture near the main house. Skipper's mom, Misty, had another foal, Christie, who was several months old. I spent every minute I could with my horses. My three shelties were with me as much as possible too and had a huge fenced yard. Once or twice a day I let them run free in one of the other pastures away from the horses. With 250 acres of mostly pasture, there was plenty of room for them to race around and play.

Chapter 8

When Emily and I were working for the airlines, we would stop in at The Hummingbird Café on the way home after work to have a drink. We made friends with Marty, the owner, there and he became like family to us.

Many artists got their break and were discovered in this café. I was lucky enough to be one of them. One night at open mic night, Emily had pushed me to sing and a producer happened to be in the audience. He saw something in my music and told Marty I had "it". He gave me a tentative recording contract with Big Dream Nashville if I ever decided to go on the road to promote my music. I was quite happy simply performing at The Hummingbird and other small clubs in Nashville when I felt like it. Marty had been constantly on my case to sign the contract and go the route to become a famous artist. He knew I could accomplish whatever I decided to do.

Emily thought so too. She and I had been friends since we were in grammar school. We were best buds and we each had each other's back especially where men were concerned. We made sure the other's head was on straight, especially with so many cowboys around.

I had trusted her with a secret about my past that I hadn't shared with anyone. A long time ago an old friend and I went to a dude ranch outside of Gatlinburg. She had been there before and told me how much fun it was. We rode the horses during the day and enjoyed the live music at night. I was young and impressionable (stupid) and fell in love with one of the cowboys. He was sweet and handsome and said all the right things. We returned the following weekend and he made a big deal of how glad he was to see me. His name was Tommy and he was a bareback bronc rider. The cowboys all stayed in a common bunkhouse and he asked me if I would like to visit him there. My friend was off somewhere with someone else so I thought sure, why not. We were sitting on his bunk by ourselves and he asked me if I would like a drink of Old Grand Dad whiskey. I told him I didn't drink but he said he'd put some ginger ale in it to make it taste better. Long story short, when he started to kiss me and go further, I didn't stop him. I thought he really liked me and had no idea this was just a game they all played. When it was over, he acted like he wanted me to leave so I gathered my things and walked out. He didn't even say goodbye. I was devastated and upset at my poor judgment. My friend was sitting outside waiting for me and shook her head when she realized what had happened. My head hurt from the whiskey and I just wanted to get out of there. We got in the car and drove three hours back home to Nashville and I never told anyone except her and Emily about it. Emily made me understand that we all make mistakes and as long as I didn't get pregnant, I should just forget it. It has haunted me to this day.

—

Chapter 9

It was a busy time of year at the ranch. Located about thirty miles south of Nashville, lots of tourists visited for a taste of the Tennessee countryside and to experience a real working quarter horse ranch. This particular morning the weather was beautiful and some were waiting in line for a trail ride. A wrangler joined me as we took them on an hour-long ride through the fields and over by the creek. We walked most of the way, as these were novice riders with no real riding experience. I enjoyed chatting with the guests as we went along. I loved this part of my job.

With 30 brood mares, a stallion named Bucky, and foals running around next to their mares, there was plenty of work to be done on the ranch. Jake, a part-time wrangler, pretty much was in charge of the breeding program, watching the mares to see when they came into heat. If there was any extra free time, he and Ryan were welcome to go down the road to the big farms where the famous people lived and earn a little extra money helping them out.

In a free moment I told Emily, "I just love this time of year here on the ranch. Spring is beginning, foals have been born and the breeding season is over. I love seeing the mares with their babies alongside them up in the hilly part of the pasture. It is so pretty there with the creek running through."

Emily agreed and we decided to take a walk and enjoy the scenery. We passed by the food truck throwing out hay and grain to the horses. Ryan yelled at us as he and Jake drove by. Jake had his hat off and you could see his dark blond hair blowing in the breeze.

"Emily," I laughed, "I swear Ryan has a thing for you. You should go have a drink with him or something!"

She answered, "Just too busy to start anything right now, you know how it is."

Chapter 10

With so many horses to be taken care of daily, the cowboys didn't have much free time. The horses in training and the pregnant mares spent the night in the barns with daily exercise and turnouts. When a foal was due to be born, it wasn't unusual for a cowboy or two and a girlfriend to hang out in the barn at night waiting and watching. I certainly was not above doing this but at least tried to be discreet. Somebody always caught on and gossiped about it the next morning. I swore I'd never have a cowboy for a boyfriend because of what happened at the dude ranch. I did like Chance but kept him at arm's length most of the time. He seemed to be enthralled with me however, and kept trying to convince me to take him seriously.

My phone pinged when we got back to the ranch. It was Chance,

"Hey beautiful, how are you?"

I smiled to myself at the compliment and responded, "Feeling better and better, thanks."

"How about going out to dinner tonight to celebrate your rodeo title?"

My heart jumped a little as I answered, "Sure, I'd love to."

Emily had a big smile on her face and said it was about time I gave the boy some attention. I wondered what to wear and what restaurant we'd go to. He would probably choose The Trick Pony, his favorite place. They had live music and a huge dance floor.

I chose a favorite dressy tee and long colorful skirt to wear. I had upgraded my shoe style and now wore a dressier low boot instead of cowboy boots when I went out. My blonde hair had recently been highlighted and trimmed to shoulder length. All I had to do was add a little makeup and put in my green contacts. I told Emily to come down and meet us but she had something else to do. I thought it strange that she couldn't come. She told me to have a great time.

I couldn't help but be excited. Chance was tall and handsome, always wore a cowboy hat and boots and wouldn't be caught dead in anything but Wranglers. His brown hair was trimmed nicely and there was a twinkle in his brown eyes. His smile was what attracted me to him. It was genuine and would light up a room.

Chapter 11

Chance picked me up in his white Ford F-250 and he was right on time. He opened the door for me and helped me climb in. It was pretty quiet around the ranch at this time of day. Marty and Dixie were at The Hummingbird. As we left, Ryan was feeding the horses and bringing some of them up to the barns. He waved as we drove by. It was a beautiful hot night with a full bright moon in Tennessee. I loved living here.

Franklin was a small town compared to Nashville. Even so, there were always lots of tourists around and they loved to go out to eat.

This restaurant was very popular and the parking lot was almost full. Chance said there must be something going on for it to be so busy on a weeknight. He took my hand as we walked from the parking lot to the main entrance. I normally would shy away but for some reason tonight I didn't. He held the door for me saying, "after you" and as I walked in, I realized something was going on. The lights flashed on and off and everyone yelled "SURPRISE!"

Chance grabbed and hugged me at the same time as everyone rushed to congratulate me. There was a huge banner with the words CONGRATULATIONS BECKY! MISS RODEO

TENNESSEE!! that went all the way across the room behind the bar. I was totally blown away. Emily, who had said she was too busy to come, laughed and said she'd never have missed this for anything.

Eventually it calmed down a little and everyone took their seats for dinner. My close friends sat at two tables by the bar. It looked like Ryan was going to sit with Emily at our table, which made me smile. I wanted to know whose idea this was and eventually I learned Chance and Emily set up the whole thing. No surprise there. It looked like about thirty friends were invited. Marty and Dixie made the rounds and welcomed everyone. I didn't know it at the time but they paid for everything, even the dessert.

It was a lovely party with excellent food and lots of laughs. Everyone told stories about their younger days in Nashville. Through it all Chance held my hand under the table and never took his eyes away from me. I was definitely feeling something for him that surpassed the nights in the barn waiting for foals to be born. This was different. Chance proposed a toast and everyone raised their glasses towards me. I was very embarrassed but in a good way. He made me feel special.

The band showed up around 8:30 and set up. I knew these guys because they were my band when I sang at The Hummingbird. Just three great guys that loved country music. Chance asked me to dance and I accepted. The others on the dance floor smiled as we joined them. It felt good to have his arms around me. I felt safe and protected. This was something new for me. I had had lots of dates that went nowhere. This was my first attempt at a serious relationship.

It was just a matter of time until Emily had to ask if anyone wanted me to sing something. I shook my head but everyone started to clap and I was stuck. She even brought one of my hats and my guitar because she knew I wouldn't sing without them. I took a deep breath, got up and walked over to the small stage. I turned and smiled at everyone and put the guitar over my shoulder. I thanked them all for coming and for making this night so special. I gave Kenny, my bandleader, a high five and we started the intro to my signature song, SUPERSTAR, like we had done hundreds of times before. Music was my passion. Aside from the ranch and the animals, this was what I wanted to do with my life. There was applause and when it was over we all took a bow. Chance looked so proud of me. I couldn't wait to get back to him. Emily was just bubbling over. I hugged her and thanked her for putting this together.

We stayed for a while but I knew I shouldn't overdo so I asked Chance to take me home. We held hands all the way to the ranch and he kissed me goodnight. He asked if he could come in but I said "not tonight." I kissed him back and thanked him for a wonderful evening. I could feel myself falling for him and even though I really tried to rein in my feelings, it was no use. He told me he'd call tomorrow. He watched to be sure I got in the house safely and I blew him a kiss as I opened the door.

Chapter 12

The next morning after we rehashed the party the night before, Emily pulled out the questions from the doctor. My next appointment was coming up. She was bound and determined not to forget to ask me anything. It didn't seem like anything had changed. Marty wanted to know when I could come back to perform. My fans wanted to see me, to be assured that I was well and recovered even though my memory loss was not shared in the media.

Emily remembered The ELLEN Show had sent me an email regarding a show she was doing about women starting new careers later in life. I did remember this but I had forgotten that I was supposed to contact them about going to LA. Emily said she would send a follow up email and ask when the show was scheduled and if they still wanted me to participate. She would tell them about my accident and apologize for not contacting them sooner.

Within a day she heard back that the show had already been recorded and aired. There was a possibility they would do a follow-up because the first one was such a big hit. The crew would come here. I wouldn't have to fly to LA. They would be in touch.

Meanwhile, Chance called to see if I wanted to join him for breakfast or lunch...or both. I smiled and told him I had a busy morning with guests but that I could squeeze in breakfast.

He replied, "Great, Becky, see you around ten."

He hung up before I could say anything, like he was getting another call. I wondered if someone was booking him for the rodeo this weekend. He put on such a great show. I finished working with a couple mares and their foals and led them back to the pasture with the others. I felt almost guilty for going to breakfast. I hurried and changed my shirt and washed my hands. I knew he would be on time.

Chance came down the road to the main house in his monster truck. He just had it washed so it gleamed in the sun. I climbed in and slid over next to him.

"Any particular reason you want to have breakfast?" I asked.

He said "Yup, it's about time you learned some stuff about me so you know what you're getting into."

What's he talking about, I wondered, even as I realized I didn't know a thing about his growing up years or his family. We parked on the street in Franklin by the diner. He started to talk even before the coffee came. It was like he was on a mission or something. I settled into the booth and listened, really listened.

Chapter 13

Chance and his sister, Trisha, were born and raised on a farm in Upstate New York. Their parents, Barbara and Sonny Mason, were airline people who both had careers working for a commercial airline. Sonny joined the Air Force out of high school and learned to fly fighter jets. When he retired he continued his aviation career as a commercial pilot. Barbara was a first class flight attendant when the two met on a cross-country trip and married within months. It was love at first sight.

Chance explained that the family moved to Franklin a few years before. His mother had had enough of the harsh winters up north and it was just as easy for her husband to be based in Nashville where he picked up his commercial trips. His sister Trisha who was two years younger than me, decided to stay in New York where she became a successful trauma nurse at a big hospital. She had visited the family in Tennessee but hated the hot summers and preferred the change of seasons in her hometown. Chance explained that he graduated from college but decided he wanted to work at rodeos as a performer, which was where the nickname Chance came from. His real name was Adam.

He said when they arrived in Nashville the family made friends with Marty and Dixie at The Hummingbird. There was a house for sale with some land nearby which Marty helped them buy. There was an apartment in the finished basement, which became Chance's man cave. One day he saw me sitting at the counter a few feet away. He felt his heart leap and knew I was going to be special in his life. I blushed and said that was the nicest thing anyone had ever said to me. He was concerned he may have said too much but I told him I was very touched by his words.

We were then interrupted by a friend of his named Stitch. I thought, does everyone have a nickname? He shook my hand.

"Are you and Chance an item now?" he asked. I glanced over at Chance who was clearly annoyed.

He answered, "It is none of your business but yes, we are definitely an item."

"I'm sorry if I was rude," said Stitch, "but I wonder what Carrie would say about this. "I thought Chance was going to get up and run him off. After Stitch left I asked what he was talking about.

"It's a story for another time." Of course I wanted to know what he was talking about, but I had to get back to the ranch. And who was Carrie?

Chance was strangely quiet on the way home and I could tell something was weighing on him. Ryan started teasing Chance when we arrived back at the ranch. I told him to leave Chance alone and help me take out the two trail rides that had been rescheduled. The horses were saddled and the guests were waiting. After I kissed Chance goodbye, I waved as he took off up the driveway.

Chapter 14

I called Chance the next morning and asked him to meet me at the local diner for coffee. There I asked him what Stich was talking about. He hesitated at first but decided to just come out and tell me. I knew Chance must have had other girlfriends, after all he was in his late thirties, but I didn't expect or imagine this.

Before his family moved to Tennessee, he had a girlfriend he'd met in college. Her name was Carrie and they dated on and off for a few years. He was never into her but she was crazy about him and wanted them to share their life together. One day she announced she was pregnant. She wanted them to get married but he said no. He told her he would help her and support the child if she wanted to keep it, but that was all. Then his family moved to Tennessee and she stayed in New York. A baby girl was born with her mom's black hair and hazel eyes. He flew up to see her and the baby the day after she was born. Her name was Cassidy. Chance paused to see how I was reacting to this. I was somewhat in shock so I just nodded and told him to keep going.

He would see his daughter as much as he could and she spent summers in Franklin. There was nothing between him and Carrie except co-parenting. Carrie constantly hounded him to rekindle their relationship so they could make a home for Cassidy. He was not interested. His daughter was four years old.

He thought he'd better tell me because they would be coming to visit him soon. Carrie had friends in Nashville but they would stay at his parent's home. It was awkward but he always tolerated Carrie for the sake of their daughter. Cassidy loved seeing him at the rodeos.

All I could muster to say was, "Do you have a picture of her?" He took out his wallet and showed me a picture of a beautiful child.

"Becky, this doesn't have to change anything between us. Please. What are you thinking?"

I was thinking I had to talk to Emily. She'll never believe this. I told Chance I needed time to process. He told me to take all the time I needed. We walked out together and he hugged me and told me to call him when I could.

"Please Becky, we can work this out," he pleaded.

I drove home with my head spinning. Emily was there and met me at the driveway. She said I looked like I had seen a ghost.

Chapter 15

Level-headed Emily. Always has been. Always will be. She listened to the tale of the little girl and said, "So what? Do you honestly think there's a thirty/something out there with no baggage? Especially one who looks like Chance? I'd be more worried about the girlfriend. She sounds a little loony tunes to me."

I smiled at Emily's description. I had calmed down and gotten over the initial shock of Chance having a daughter. Emily pointed out that if I fell in love with him, it wouldn't matter. "So for now just get over it."

Later that day, I saw the monster truck parked by the stables. What was Chance doing at the ranch? I noticed Skipper had a saddle on and so did Barney, one of the other horses. Chance knocked on my door.

"Hi there, Becky, thought you might join me for a ride. It's a beautiful day." I smiled and agreed, walking toward the horses.

"Who'd you get to saddle the horses?" I asked.

"Ryan wasn't busy so he said he'd do it. No problem," he answered.

We rode off to the end of the dirt road by the pastures and cut through to Chance's house.

"My parents are in Dallas on a trip so no one's home. Thought you might like a cup of coffee."

We dismounted and tied Skipper and Barney to a tree where they could eat grass.

I had never been in Chance's house before and was a little leery at first but he was a perfect gentleman. It was obvious he wanted to talk to me in private about his daughter. I started the conversation.

"When is Cassidy coming and when can I meet her? Maybe she'd like to see all the foals at the ranch."

Chance responded, "She's coming next week and she'd love that, Becky. Thanks."

"Well, I've got a busy week so just bring her over when you can."

We finished our coffee and rode the horses the long way back to the ranch. I was still feeling a little unsettled and knew Chance and I needed more time to talk about this. When I mentioned it he agreed and said he'd come back over later if I wasn't busy.

When I went into my house, I noticed my tiara on the table. It reminded me how every once in a while I'm asked to appear somewhere in the state as Miss Rodeo Tennessee. I loved being part of different functions and meeting such wonderful people. It was an honor to represent the great state of Tennessee and I took the responsibility very seriously.

Meanwhile 1000 miles north in the middle of one of the Finger Lakes in New York State, Carrie sat on a beautiful cruiser with her mother, Allison and her daughter Cassidy. She had rented the boat for the day complete with food, drink and driver. The homes along the shoreline were expensive and beautiful. There were jet skiers zooming past and people waving from boats going by. The water was clear and blue just like the sky.

She was telling Cassidy about their trip the next week to Nashville. She told her to be extra nice to her daddy so that maybe he would come up for a visit after they returned home. They didn't call him Chance. They called him Adam.

Carrie told her mother, "It is just a matter of time before Adam finds someone and settles down. Then it will be too late. He belongs with us. He always has."

Chapter 16

Marty was on his way home from the club because a buyer was coming to look at a two year old green broke filly. I had called him because this was such an important sale. Ryan had been working with her and it looked like she had the potential to be a great barrel horse.

Right when the buyer showed up, Marty arrived and Chance pulled into the driveway. I waved at him and then climbed into his truck. He was surprised because he thought we were staying at the ranch.

"Hell, no," I said when he asked what was going on. "There're too many people around here. Let's go over to your place where we can have some privacy."

Chance smiled. "No argument here," he said as he turned around and headed back up the driveway.

When we arrived we went into the kitchen and Chance made coffee. I sat at the coffee bar and looked out at the beautiful yard with a view of the mountains in the distance. For someone who talked a lot I couldn't think of a thing to say. Chance picked up the ball and started to talk about Cassidy and how he couldn't wait till I met her.

"You seem sure it's a good idea?" I asked.

"Absolutely," Chance answered, "You two are going to be best friends."

We talked about how she was growing up fast and how much he missed her. When I mentioned Carrie, he just said he'd rather not talk about her.

"She's a good mother but I don't think she's a very nice person." So I knew there was nothing more to be said on the subject.

Chance mentioned that Marty had called him that morning with a proposition for him.

"What on earth?" I couldn't imagine what this was about.

"He wants me to travel with you, to be a bodyguard of sorts, if it's ok with you. I can fly for free because of my father's passes. What do you think Becky?"

I was trying not to jump up and down with excitement. What a great idea. I tried to be calm.

"He must trust you a lot to ask you to do this. We'd have to try to see if it would work out."

"Oh I'm sure it'll work out," Chance winked. He put his arm around me. "It's up to you Becky."

I smiled and said, "It's a great idea."

We spent another hour just talking small talk about the music business and rodeo gossip when I decided I better head back to the ranch. When I got up to leave, Chance kissed me and said he wished I could stay. My heart was pounding but I just told him, "another time."

When we got back to the ranch, the new buyer was loading the filly into his truck. I shook his hand and wished him luck. She was a favorite of mine so I was extra glad she was getting a good home. Chance walked over to talk to Marty and I hesitated for a minute until Chance called me over to join them. I told Marty I was glad he asked Chance to watch out for me. Chance smiled and said no one would bother me on his watch.

Marty went into the house and I stayed there with Chance for a few minutes. I really didn't want to call it a night but I had a recording session first thing in the morning. We promised we would spend some time together the next day. Chance said we should go to dinner just the two of us. I told him it was a date! We hugged and he got into his truck and left. I watched him go up the driveway and turn right onto Highway 96.

Slowly I walked into the house. My mind was jumbled up with everything going on. One thing I knew for sure. I was falling for this guy and I'd have to decide sooner than later if we would sleep together. This was a huge decision and I wanted to be sure I knew what I was doing. Emily wasn't around to talk to but I was pretty sure she would tell me to go for it. I saw lights coming down the driveway and realized Emily was coming home.

She parked her car and I saw the passenger side door open. Ryan got out and walked around to the driver's side. I felt like I shouldn't be watching but I couldn't help myself. Emily got out of the car and the two of them walked toward the bunkhouse. I smiled to myself and said there must be something in the water. It's a good thing this bunkhouse is remodeled. This one even had running water and a shower!

Chapter 17

The next morning I was up having coffee when Emily blew in. She asked me what I was doing.

"We have to draw straws to see who talks first," I answered.

"You saw us?"

"I only saw you walking toward the bunkhouse. What happened after that, I have no idea." We both collapsed in giggles.

"Wait," she said. "What are YOU talking about?"

I explained, "I have a decision to make but have a pretty good idea what you're going to tell me."

Emily waited for an explanation.

"Chance asked me to go to dinner tonight," I explained. "We're going to the Red Blossom in Nashville. He doesn't know I picked the restaurant."

Emily's eyes were twinkling. "It's a really nice place. What's the occasion as if I didn't know?" She laughed as she figured it out.

We both had to start our day so we said we'd try to meet up later, no promises. After hugs, we both walked out and got into our cars. I followed her for a mile or so and then turned north towards Nashville.

What would I wear for my date with Chance? I chose a pretty yellow sundress with my new white booties. The skirt was short and I checked in the mirror to be sure I was covered. No cowboy hat, I let my hair fall to my shoulders. I very seldom wore makeup except when I performed but I added a little especially around my eyes.

I was more nervous than I realized and was glad we chose an early time for dinner. The restaurant was popular with hometown folk and I wanted to be sure we'd get a booth. We had agreed to stop over at The Hummingbird after dinner for a drink.

Emily yelled, "Have a good evening you two!" as we drove up the driveway. Chance wore his wranglers and cowboy hat, of course. He dressed up a little with a blue cowboy shirt and his rodeo buckle on his belt. He looked very handsome. He reached into the back seat to give me flowers when he arrived. He knew daisies were my favorite. I quickly ran into the house and put them in water on the counter. It was very sweet of him. I climbed back in the truck and gave him a kiss. Later we parked on the street and walked about a block to the restaurant. If he was nervous, it didn't show and I was nervous enough for both of us. I couldn't wait to have a bushwhacker. Chance had a Yazoo in a huge glass.

Once we were seated, I relaxed a little and enjoyed being alone with him. There had always been people around before. This restaurant was known for its seafood and we ordered a giant seafood platter, which we shared. It wasn't long before we were laughing and enjoying every moment. It was a major thing for me to be with a man who made me laugh and Chance had me in stitches. The food was delicious and neither of us wanted dessert or coffee. We left arm in arm and drove the short distance to The Hummingbird. Kelsey, a striking redhead, was behind the bar and was very happy to see us. Marty came out from the back to say hello. I told Chance I thought he really liked him. It was open mic night and I enjoyed seeing the new faces. At one point, Chance leaned over and whispered, "Let's get out of here," and he didn't have to ask me twice.

Chapter 18

We drove the 30 miles back to Chance's house in a flash. When we got inside, he slammed the door and started to kiss me. Clothes came off and we hurriedly fell onto the bed together. He was so sexy and charming. Our lovemaking was tender and passionate at the same time. When everything had calmed down, he held me and asked if we should have waited.

I said, "Hell, no, we have waited long enough."

He chuckled and said he had been waiting for years. I touched his cheek and looked deep into his eyes. I felt safe with this man and realized we were falling in love. A memory of another time tried to resurface but I pushed it away. I felt goosebumps and took that as a good sign.

We fell asleep for a little while. When we woke up, we both wished we could just stay there and not move but we had to get dressed so he could take me home. Something big was happening here. When we kissed good night, we lingered just because we didn't want to leave each other. He was welcome to stay at the house with me if he wanted. I think Emily had made herself scarce but he decided to go back to his parent's home in case she came back. We said goodnight and hugged each other.

My senses were alive and I couldn't wait to see him again.

"I'll call you in the morning, Honey, sleep tight." His sweet words. I slowly got out of the monster truck and turned around for a moment to smile at him before I went into the house. So much emotion welling up in my heart. I was glad Emily was not around for now.

Next morning I was off to rehearse at The Hummingbird. The streets were almost deserted in downtown Nashville. There were a few brave souls out walking around in a daze holding coffee cups. Marty had called the photographer for the cover of the second CD. He'd be there any minute with makeup and a hair stylist. If it were up to me I'd pull my hair back in a ponytail and be done with it. One emergency phone call to Emily (I forgot my red cowboy boots), and I was ready.

The Hummingbird was a different kind of club. Along with the stage, there were a few tables with mics set up for singers. It catered to new and inexperienced artists, giving them confidence as they gained experience. I remembered how scared I was the first time I was talked into open mic night. I owe this club for giving me my start in country music.

The pictures turned out great. My favorite was the one with me standing next to a saddle with my guitar, a short skirt, my white hat and my red boots. My name was printed in white against a blue background. "Meet Miss Becky Steele." "SUPERSTAR" was printed across the top in dark blue lettering. It was very classy. Marty chose this one too. So this part was done. My phone pinged right in the middle of a rehearsal. It was Chance. I would have to call him back.

Next I had to learn two new songs. We took a break for a couple days and said we'd meet in a day or two. Marty had the sheet music and gave it to me to take home. It was hard to concentrate on the music when last night was front and center in my mind.

When I got home, there were flowers outside the main door. Emily teased me, "Now why do you suppose somebody sent them?" She said my face gave everything away and she was glad I was so happy.

The rehearsals were going well and we could actually do a run through of all three songs without screwing things up. These songs would be performed Friday night at The Hummingbird. Stay tuned.

The next day Chance called to tell me Cassidy and her mother would be arriving a week from Saturday. His parents came home that morning. He said they would be staying at his parent's house. I invited Cassidy to stay with us sometimes too.

I asked him to please come to The Hummingbird on Friday to see what we'd been working on. He said he wouldn't miss it and that he would be glad to take me.'

"I'll pick you up at 8," he said. "Miss you. See you soon."

"I miss you too," I replied.

In the morning we had one final rehearsal. I thanked the guys for their hard work. The two songs the producer chose were upbeat and fun. Against the eerie sound of SUPERSTAR, they were a nice contrast.

After rehearsal I drove home and went for a walk with my dogs. I remembered a man's face in my mind when I was singing SUPERSTAR. Why did I have goosebumps and who was he?

Chapter 19

I had a voicemail from my doctor clearing me to sing. I sent Marty a text telling him to expect me on Friday night. I had time to prepare. I was glad part of my life was coming back. I missed singing and being on stage. Emily asked me out of the blue if I remembered being married very young and did I ever tell Chance? I vaguely remembered being married and living in Miami but I couldn't remember if I told Chance.

Friday night came fast and I was busy getting dressed. Chance was picking me up in half an hour. Why was I nervous? I had done this so many times. Julie made sure all my clothes and accessories were ready. I hadn't performed in about a month, so I was a little out of practice. I decided on a white outfit with silver sparkles. I put on more makeup than usual so I wouldn't look so pale. Chance blew the horn when he got here and I went out and climbed into his truck. I told myself I was more excited than nervous. Marty had put my guitar in the back of the truck. I was ready.

My goodness, the parking lot was overflowing! Marty had written, "Beck's Back" on the marque. We ducked in the back door. People swarmed us and Chance had to do damage control. I hid in the back room until Kenny came and told me it was time to go on. I was only singing

SUPERSTAR. It was an awesome moment for me to walk up those steps onto the stage, it was almost like the first time. My voice was strong and I could feel the emotion of the words. I noticed my eyes were tearing up and I felt goosebumps. What was that all about? I saw the image of the same man in my mind smiling at me. I shook my head to clear it and took a bow in response to the applause. Everyone was very kind. Chance came up on stage and put his arm around me to guide me back to our table. We sat there and had a drink. He asked me what was wrong. I didn't know how to answer so I said, "Nothing, I'm just emotional." He looked at me with concern. Emily had slipped in quietly and had seen what had happened. She saw the look on my face and the tears in my eyes.

She knew I was seeing Johnny in my mind even though I didn't. She made a note to tell the doctor that some of the forgotten memories were coming back.

Chapter 20

A few weeks later, The ELLEN Show sent Emily an email asking if I was still interested in being interviewed. The second segment about women starting entertainment careers later in life would air in about three months. If I was interested they would send a crew to The Hummingbird by the end of the week. ELLEN wanted me to sing "SUPERSTAR" of course, along with my first single off the new album.

Her crew arrived in the morning three days later. I was there at The Hummingbird with Marty and my band when they arrived. It took a while to set up the sound equipment and the visual components. ELLEN would do the segment with me live. Marty had the marquee changed to read, "BECKY DOES THE ELLEN SHOW" and people started wandering in almost immediately.

I remarked to Marty, "If nothing else, all this publicity is good for business!"

He smiled, "Becky, you are the best thing that ever happened for business at The Hummingbird."

Chance arrived in time to bring me flowers and give me encouragement. I loved the way he was always so supportive. Just having him there beside me made the day perfect for me. Julie had bought a gold sparkly two-piece outfit for me to wear. I felt like a princess!

The time had come for the taping to begin. I walked out on stage as I always did, waving and smiling at the crowd. I made eye contact with Chance and smiled. Even though it was during the day, it was standing room only. The lights dimmed as ELLEN's voice came out of the speakers and her image appeared on the monitors. Everyone had their phones out taking pictures. My heart was beating so loud I swear everyone could hear it.

She asked me a few questions about my singing career and then asked me to sing "SUPERSTAR". A hush came over the room as I performed the beautiful song flawlessly.

Everyone always told me I made Karen Carpenter, the original recording artist, proud. The crowd applauded and cheered when I finished. We immediately launched into one of the new songs and everyone sang along as I immersed myself into the melody and got the crowd to clap with me. ELLEN was impressed and told me so.

Ellen thanked me for my time and started to say goodbye when she remembered something. She told me to wait just a minute as one of the crew brought out a beautiful pink autographed guitar and gave it to me. It was a very special moment and I cried as I thanked her from the bottom of my heart. She told me to keep on singing and wished me the best. The monitors and speakers were suddenly silent and ELLEN was gone.

Chance was right by my side as I walked off the stage after thunderous applause from the audience. He hugged me and told me how proud he was and how much he loved me. I squeezed his hand and teared up from all the emotion. I just couldn't believe ELLEN would be so supportive and give me a beautiful guitar. I asked Chance to take me home. I was too emotional to talk to anyone. What a day.

Emily finally came flying in through the door and hugged me. I put my arms around Chance and Emily and smiled at them. I was so grateful for their love. Marty caught me on the way out and gave me a big hug. He said, "You put The Hummingbird on everyone's lips."

Most of the crowd had started to leave the club so no one noticed the handsome man in a sweatshirt and ball cap standing by the fire exit. Johnny stood quietly in the shadows as he watched Becky's big moment with ELLEN. He quickly disappeared into the street before anyone recognized him.

Chapter 21

The show behind me, I took some time to concentrate on our guests and spend time outdoors in the Tennessee countryside with my horses and dogs. I knew things could get crazy and I didn't want my animals neglected. Chance was around most of the time now. It seemed perfectly natural for him to be with me whenever he wasn't working with his animals or his rodeo act. We were getting to know each other's likes and dislikes and were becoming very comfortable with each other. Even Dixie mentioned how in tune we seemed to be with each other.

I was surprised how easy it was to be with him. As rugged as he looked, he was really just a kind and gentle man. I thought I'd better mention to him that I had been married and divorced very young. I didn't want him to think I wasn't being honest but he said I had told him already and it was no big deal.

Chance's daughter would be arriving any time and he wanted to be there when she landed at the airport. He kept looking at his phone waiting for the call. I hoped all would go well with Cassidy's mom, that she wouldn't pick an argument with Chance especially when he mentioned me. I had a feeling we were in for some rough times ahead.

50

Emily and I decorated the small bedroom in our house for Cassidy. We hoped she liked the pink walls and the pink and white princess bedspread. Stars decorated the ceiling like I had when I was a little girl. There were white daisies in vases on her dresser and stuffed animals on her bed. Chance bought her a stable horse, which sat in the corner of the room. She looked almost real. What would Cassidy name her?

The plane was delayed an hour. Chance was at the airport early as usual and texted me when they were late. He asked me to call his mom and tell her he couldn't get through to her. I left a message on her voicemail and went into the house with Emily. I assumed I wouldn't hear from him until the following day when I heard the monster truck coming down the driveway. I went outside. Chance parked the truck and walked over to me and kissed me. I looked to see if there was anyone with him but he was alone. I asked him what he was doing there and he said he missed me. I asked how things were going and he said Carrie was the same bitch she's always been and Cassidy was just so precious he could eat her up. I walked out with him and told him I'd see him in the morning. We hugged and said goodnight. I couldn't wait to meet his daughter.

When I came back to the house Emily asked me if she should ask Marty if she could live in the main house. She was concerned for my privacy with Chance and now his daughter. I told her I loved living with her and hoped we could work it out. The bedrooms were at opposite ends of the ranch so privacy wouldn't be a problem. Emily made me promise to tell her if there was any reason I was uncomfortable. There was plenty of room at the main house. I wondered if she wanted to move up there.

"Emily," I said, "Cassidy will spend most of her time with Chance's parents. She probably will be here a day a week maybe. It shouldn't be a problem. I don't expect Chance will be staying here every night."

Emily smiled and said she just wanted everything to be perfect.

Don't bet on it.

Chapter 22

Emily had me up at the crack of dawn. She wanted to be sure I was dressed and ready in case Cassidy's mother came with her. I hadn't even thought of the possibility. I just assumed Chance would bring her.

I asked Ryan to take over the trail rides for the day. Chance called at 9:00 to see if it was too early to bring Cassidy over. Lollipop was saddled and waiting for her and I had a carrot in my pocket. He said they'd be right over. No mention of Carrie, so far.

She was so little you could hardly see her in the back seat of his truck. He parked and took her out of her car seat and they walked over to where I was standing. She was a beautiful child with sparkling eyes and a fun smile. She hid a little behind her father until he told her my name was Becky and I had a carrot for Lollipop. She then came right over to me and said her name was Cassidy. I asked if she was ready to ride. She had on the cutest white cowboy boots. Chance lifted her into the saddle and I told her to hang on as I walked Lollipop around. She was ecstatic and her little face shone with happiness. I must have looked like that when I was four. For a moment, I thought of my momma and remembered her taking me to a farm so I could see the horses. When Chance lifted her off, I gave her the carrot, which she in turn gave to Lollipop. She clapped her hands in glee. Chance was all smiles...until he saw Carrie coming down the driveway.

I gave Lollipop's reins to Ryan and went over and stood next to Chance. Carrie got out of the car and walked over to me with a smile on her face.

"Hi, I'm Carrie and thanks for giving my daughter a ride."

She seemed nice but Chance's body language said otherwise. She had jet black hair and for a second I had the image of a witch in my head. I excused myself by saying I had work to do with the young horses. Carrie asked if she could look around and I said of course. Out of the corner of my eye I could see Emily watching. The whole situation was tense and I couldn't wait to get away from there. I said goodbye to Cassidy and touched Chance on the arm, a gesture that did not go unnoticed. Carrie saw it and gave me a really dirty look. Emily caught up with us and told me I was needed in the house. Saved by the bell!

Chance looked like he was going to blow his top but instead he took Cassidy by the hand.

"It's time to go. Say goodbye to Becky."

She ran over to me and said, "Thank you. Can I come visit again?"

I replied, "Sure thing," and escaped into the house. Emily came right after me. I could hear Chance telling Carrie to take Cassidy back to his mom's and that he would see them later. Carrie was definitely not happy.

Emily said, "I guess she figured it out."

Chance came in the house and apologized for her rudeness.

"She asked me if we were seeing each other."

"You told her, right?" I asked.

"Yes," Chance answered.

"This is a problem," I said. "I don't know how we're going to do this if she insists on bringing Cassidy." I didn't tell him she reminded me of a witch.

I could feel the tension mounting between us. I wasn't going to let Carrie ruin things for us, which was exactly what she was trying to do.

"Come on Becky, let's go have lunch. I'll talk to her when I get back."

Chance took my hand. It was clear he wasn't as annoyed as I was.

Chapter 23

Lunch was very quiet. We would normally be chatting away with all kinds of things to share. It was like Carrie was in the middle of us. Chance told me he was going to tell her we were together and reassured me that there was no way she could interfere. He wanted to spend time with Cassidy without Carrie hanging around. She had friends to see and places to go. I asked him how she would react and he said probably not well. He said he knew my recording session was coming up and he wanted me to concentrate on it. He was going to spend the night with me no matter what. This made me smile and I told him to bring his jammies and just come over. We hugged and he said he was going to make everything all right.

We stopped at The Hummingbird to drop off my things for the morning. We were going to record in one of the biggest recording studios on music row. Even though this was my second CD, I was just as excited as I was the first time. I pushed Carrie to the back of my mind.

Our first night together in the house was everything I had hoped and dreamed of. Carrie was the furthest thing from our minds. Emily insisted on spending the night with her parents in Nashville. Julie had purchased new sheets and a new comforter in perfect relaxing colors. We drew the drapes and shut the world out. We laughed and loved and snuggled together like we had been together before, in another life? Perhaps. All I knew was we belonged together. I didn't want the night to end. I needed to get some sleep so I finally rolled over and kissed him and said goodnight. He held onto me like he was afraid I was going to leave. I told him he was stuck with me. I wasn't going anywhere.

The alarm on my phone woke us up in the morning. We stretched and said good morning and made love again.

"Now I'm going to be late," I exclaimed as I jumped into the shower while he quickly dressed. He needed to go home to get clothes. I suggested he leave some things at my place. My dogs greeted us and I quickly made coffee and went out on the porch. It was evident to me that, while this was a big deal having Chance here, no one else seemed to care.

He got in his truck and told me he'd see me at the recording studio. Emily had come back and was in my car waiting for me. We had plenty of time for my nerves to take over. Emily said she had never seen me look so good.

"This boy is good for you, Becky, you better keep him around."

"I plan to Emily," I smiled. "Yes, I sure plan to."

Chapter 24

Marty and the producer from Dream Big Nashville met us at the recording studio. They gave me a refresher course for using the microphone and headphones. There were also ear monitors so I could hear myself during the performance. I hadn't used these before.

Chance sat out in the holding area and tried not to make me nervous. When we were finished, I listened from the control room and I couldn't believe how good we sounded. Everyone was high fiving each other. The hard work had paid off.

I walked out of the recording area and met Chance. He hugged me and said how great we sounded. I asked him why he was late and he said he and Carrie got into an argument when he went home. He said he told her to leave Cassidy here with him and go back to New York if she couldn't be civil and grow up. I told Chance I hoped she'd do this because there was going to be trouble if she didn't.

Marty called me over and said I'd have to go on the road soon, just for a day or two. He didn't have a schedule yet but the destination might be Memphis.

"You'll be able to go by car. Dixie and I will probably go too but you won't even know we're there. There's a Beale Street Festival in a couple weeks with an outdoor stage. You can go on a Friday, stay over one night and return Saturday night. It would give you a lot of exposure."

I mentioned Memphis to Chance and he said he had heard of the Beale Street Festival. He said there was a lot of good music and food and that some people dress up like it's Halloween.

"We'll have a blast, Becky. I'll be with you every second to make sure you're safe from any crazy drinking people."

I told him I'd wear a ball cap and big sunglasses except when I was on stage.

Back in Nashville, Carrie was talking to her mother on the phone. "You won't believe it Mom, Chance has a girlfriend who lives on the horse ranch. She took Cassidy for a pony ride so now Cassidy thinks the girlfriend is the greatest thing ever. He told me to go back home and stay there if I don't like what's going on." Her mother commented he had a life there and it didn't include her so maybe she should come home.

Carrie said, "No way, I'm not giving up without a fight."

Her mom told her she was going to get into trouble so she'd better just come on home before she does something stupid.

Chapter 25

We spent the next two weeks trying to stay out of Carrie's orbit and I was happy when Marty said we were leaving for Memphis in two days.

We needed one-night reservations so Julie took care of this. She and Emily would share a room adjoining the room Chance and I were in. Marty and Dixie would be down the hall. The band had a huge room on the first floor and they all stayed together. The equipment was stored in a trailer in the parking lot. There were locks upon locks so everything was secure.

Carrie asked Chance more than once what hotel we were staying in. He told her it was none of her business but relented and gave her the name in case she needed him for Cassidy.

It was a three-hour drive to Memphis and we would be leaving in two days. Our reservations were at the Hampton Inn right in the heart of Beale Street. There had to be plans in place for my animals and my work had to be covered while we were gone. Emily had two extra girls to cover her at the dude ranch. We had an extra wrangler to take care of the horses. Marty had help at The Hummingbird so everything was all set there. We were ready to leave in the morning except for loading the monster truck with our personal belongings. Chance and I tried to relax and get a good night's sleep. I had a million things on my mind but when he put his arms around me, I was out like a light.

We were on the road with coffee in hand by 7 am. Traffic was light at that time of the morning. Emily and Julie were in the back with headphones to disguise the fact they were sleeping. Chance was wide awake and raring to go. I was halfway between. We were going to stop for breakfast along the way.

I wondered what was going on with Carrie but decided to just let things be and not bring it up. Chance had not mentioned her lately and I knew he had spent time with Cassidy. I hoped everything was calm. Chance was spending almost every night with me now so I assumed Carrie was livid. He leaned over at a red light and kissed me. I asked him if this was a job for him or was he happy just to be with us. He said it's a perfect world when your job is something you love to do.

We rode in silence with the radio on for a while and then it happened.

I screamed, "It's on the radio!"

SUPERSTAR came through the speakers and we all woke up, I mean really woke up. Headphones off! Oh my God, the big country music station in Nashville was playing SUPERSTAR! It wasn't the first time I had heard it on the air but it was exciting nevertheless. The announcer said this was an oldie reinvented by new artist Becky Steele. Chance pulled over at a diner down the road. This was something to celebrate. We got out of the truck and there were hugs all around. I put my ball cap and sunglasses on. Might as well get used to these.

Those goosebumps were going to town.

Chapter 26

The traffic picked up as we neared Memphis. There were a lot of people going to this festival! The hotel was easy to find and we were checked in in no time. The rooms were bright and spacious. Everything on the streets and on the buildings was painted in bright festive colors. We got a map so we could find the stage easily and saw that it was in a common area about two blocks away. There was room to park behind it so the guys took the trailer over there and left it. I lost track of Marty and Dixie but I knew they were close by. I was scheduled to perform in a rotation of new artists. I changed into jeans and boots and a colorful tee. This certainly was not a dress up affair. I took off my ball cap and replaced it with one of my cowboy hats. Emily was in charge of my guitar and she promised to have it on stage with me.

What a collection of all kinds of people roaming the streets! Most had a glass of their favorite beverage in hand. Chance held onto me to keep me with him. I noticed some clowns in the crowd, which was strange. What were they doing there?

The stage crew had started to set up and were going to do a sound check in a few minutes. I wandered over there thinking I should be on stage. My band was already tuning up. We had decided to do SUPERSTAR first and then lead into the upbeat numbers.

Chance and I were standing in front of the stage when I noticed one of the clowns staring at me. Chance figured it was just a fan trying to get close. It kind of creeped me out. I wasn't a fan of clowns. He told me not to fret because he was watching everything. There was also a team of security people surrounding the stage. They gave Chance an All Access pass so he could go wherever he wanted. Julie and Emily wandered over with a drink and asked if I needed anything. I said I was ready whenever it was my turn. I stepped over to the side to be near Chance and almost bumped into one of those creepy clowns. What was it doing so close to the stage?

Chapter 27

Finally they called my name and I smiled and walked up the steps. Emily handed me my guitar. Kenny gave me the signal and started the haunting intro of SUPERSTAR.

I started to sing and the words just came out with no direction from me. I closed my eyes for a second and saw an image of a military man. I quickly regained my concentration and finished the song. We performed the other numbers and the crowd erupted into cheers and applause. I took a bow and quickly walked down the steps to Chance. He asked me if I was ok. I told him I kept seeing a vision of a man and I have no idea who it is. People were crowding around me and Chance pulled me to the side.

"Who do you think the man is?" he asked.

I answered, "I have no idea but it only happens when I sing SUPERSTAR. Weird, isn't it? Must be something from my past I can't remember."

Emily heard us talking and made a mental note to tell the doctor I saw the man again.

We all walked around for a while looking at the different items for sale and watching the people mill around. Tomorrow's show would start at noon. Chance and I both said we couldn't wait to go home. This was no surprise on my end. I had told Marty I didn't want to go on the road but my contract locked me in for a few dates as soon as we recorded the CD. You can't sell records if you don't perform at live shows. It's just the way the music industry works.

It was the strangest thing. Everywhere I looked I saw a clown looking at me. At first I thought it was just one but Emily counted four. What did they want? Chance kept them away from me and made sure I wasn't bothered. He thought it was just some goofy fans trying to get pictures or something.

The next day we set up and I was called first to perform. We did three songs, which were big fan favorites. One of them reminded me of a time I couldn't quite remember and brought a tear to my eye. There must be something about these sad songs that hits a nerve with women.

Soon the show was over and we were packed up and on the road. Marty and Dixie were right behind us as we followed the equipment trailer. We stopped along the way to have dinner and called the weekend a big success. Chance couldn't wait to get home to see Cassidy and I missed my animals. We could see the Smoky Mountains in the distance as we got closer and closer to Nashville. I loved seeing the "Welcome to Nashville" sign. Those clowns were becoming a distant memory.

Chapter 28

Cassidy was all excited because her father told her there was a rodeo over the weekend. She wanted to know if I was going to ride Skipper. It would be my first competition since the accident

"Yes, I'm going to ride Skipper if you'll cheer for us. Will you?" I asked.

She was so cute. She answered, "Of course Becky, but I have to cheer for my daddy too."

There were ten entries in the barrel racing competition. There usually were more entrants. I wondered why so few entered and I mentioned it to Chance.

"You are just too hard to beat," he said.

Laughing I said, "Let's take Cassidy shopping and get her some new clothes to wear to the rodeo. Would she like to shop with us?"

Chance answered, "She would love to. Blue is her favorite color."

"When you pick her up, don't say anything. Let's surprise her." I told him. Chance hugged me and said how sweet this was.

I was really looking forward to taking Cassidy shopping. I really hadn't been around too many little children. She was at such a cute age. Four is adorable.

When Chance got to the ranch, he unbuckled Cassidy's car seat and she ran to me.

"Hi Becky! What are we going to do today?" she asked.

"Hey Cassidy, how would you like to go shopping with us? Maybe you'd like something new to wear to the rodeo this weekend!"

She was so excited. "Daddy, can we go, please?"

I could see Chance melt when she asked him anything.

"Sure thing, let's go on down to the western store in Nashville. They've got the prettiest clothes." In the back of my mind, I remembered a shopping trip when I was little with my momma. She bought me my first cowboy boots. I loved them and wore them everywhere.

Cassidy grabbed my hand and pulled me over to the truck. "C'mon Becky, let's go!" Her enthusiasm was contagious and I was looking forward to this. Chance got in the truck and off we went. Not one mention was made of her mother. It was just the three of us together. This felt right. We let her choose her clothes and she picked adorable things, a light blue snap shirt and scarf and a navy short skirt with a navy belt. She chose a new white hat. She said she wanted to look like me. How cute. Chance had the clerk take our picture in front of the store. I was becoming very attached to this little girl.

Carrie had decided to fly back to Upstate New York and leave Cassidy with Chance for a couple of weeks. He was surprised and so was I. He said she must have had an ulterior motive because this was something she would never have done. I didn't care why she was leaving. I was just glad she was.

Chance brought Cassidy and picked me up the morning of the rodeo. Cassidy looked so cute all dressed up in blue. Ryan had the trailer set up for Skipper and was taking him over to the rodeo grounds. Marty and Dixie were going to watch Cassidy while Chance performed and I rode in the barrel racing. Chance's crew was taking care of his animals. They were expecting a huge crowd.

Emily and Julie were by my side making sure I didn't forget anything. I was a little nervous about running the barrels but I knew I'd be okay once we got out there. I proudly led the procession into the Franklin arena and had a brief flashback of the bulls running loose and the accident. I pushed it out of my mind and smiled and waved at the crowd. I could see Cassidy in the stands waving and cheering.

Chance came around after the procession and wished me luck. I kissed him and told him to be careful doing all the fancy stuff he does. The events had started and before long it was my turn to run the barrels.

I told Skipper "Let's go!" He was so ready. We had a good run, but I thought we were just a little off. We'd have to wait to see our time. Cassidy really enjoyed watching us.

The winners were eventually announced for the barrel racing and just like I thought, it wasn't our best run. We came in second. I took the time to congratulate the winner who was very happy and excited. I waved at Cassidy before taking Skipper into the holding area.

Chance was incredible as usual and you could hear Cassidy yelling, "Go Daddy!" as he performed all his tricks. The bulls were securely tied this time so there weren't any problems. He got a really big standing round of applause.

Marty and Dixie brought Cassidy to see us after we were finished. Her little face shone with happiness as her father put her up on Skipper for a short ride. She looked so little on such a big horse. Dixie told us she was cooking dinner for everyone so she would see all of us in a couple hours. She had hired people to help because there were so many of us. It was certainly something to look forward to.

We all just went back to the ranch to chill out for a few hours. It was nice to not have to be anywhere or do anything. We sat outside under the trees and admired the beautiful scenery. Chance and Ryan played frisbee and Cassidy just hung out with me.

Emily and Julie were invited to the dinner too and I wondered where we were going to put everyone. I looked over to the other side of the house and there was Ryan and Chance moving picnic tables into the shade. It looked like we were going to have a picnic. I was glad Dixie hired help. I asked her what was on the menu for dinner.

She said, "Everyone's favorite, chicken and dumplings, black-eyed peas, mashed potatoes, collard greens, cornbread and peach pie for dessert. The "peach pie" rang a bell in my head but again I couldn't remember why. Everyone enjoyed our outdoor feast and complemented Dixie on the cooking. She said the help did most of it.

After dinner Emily obviously wanted to tell me something. I was trying to just relax after such a big meal.

She put her hand on my arm and said, "I've got an idea. Why don't you and I jump on a plane and go over to Hilton Head for a day or two. Maybe being there will help you remember. We can check out the house Marty bought for all of us to stay in. It was so nice of him." I thought about what she said for a minute and decided it was a good idea.

"Let's go, Emily, maybe in a few weeks? I'm really busy now."

She smiled and said, "Okay, it's a plan."

I told her we would have a chance to talk there. I wanted to know more about all the times I still couldn't remember.

Chapter 29

The next few weeks flew by as I chose the nine songs for my album and had the arrangements written. We actually recorded a couple of them and things were on track for the others.

Out of the blue one day Cassidy asked Chance when her mother was coming back because she didn't want to go back home. She wanted to stay here with us. Chance said he didn't know but that he would call and find out. He went into the house to call and came back out a few minutes later as white as a sheet. I motioned for Emily to take Cassidy over to see Lollipop so I could talk to Chance.

"What's wrong? You look upset."

Chance quietly said, "There's a problem. Apparently Carrie has been using drugs and she overdosed last night. Her mother found her unconscious. She's in the hospital right now and will have to go into rehab. This is pretty serious." Chance said Allison wanted to know if it was okay for Cassidy to stay here while her mother was recuperating. "I'll be right back. I've got to go talk to my folks," Chance said as he got into his truck.

Emily saw him leave and came over to see what had happened. I quietly said it looked like Cassidy would be staying here with Chance for a while. Emily said, "If it's anything to do with her mother, I knew there was something strange about her. She's probably the one behind the clowns at the festival."

"It's a lot more serious than that," I said, "Carrie overdosed on opioids and her mother found her unconscious in the bathroom."

Chance was back in ten minutes. Of course his Mom and Dad said Cassidy could stay there with them when she wasn't with him. My life was about to change drastically and in a good way.

"What are you going to tell Cassidy?" I wanted to know.

Chance answered, "I'll just say her Mom is sick and tell her that she's going to be staying with us for a while. Wait Becky, is this okay with you?"

I put my arm around his shoulder. "Of course I'm fine with this. She's become very important to me and I hope she will be happy here."

Chance said, "She will be beyond happy. I'll tell her today."

Chance decided to take Cassidy with us when we went out for pizza. This was a special treat, as she didn't have it very often. He very gently told her about her mother being sick and asked her if she'd like to stay with him here in Tennessee. She felt bad about her Mom but couldn't contain her happiness about staying here with us. She wanted to be sure she could stay at the ranch with me too. I wondered when Chance would tell her she had her own room. He thought we should get a head start so we dropped by his Mom's for clothes and essentials for her. She had her own little suitcase, which she carried into the house.

I realized right away how Chance's and my private time had been affected by this change, but he swore we would make up for it. It would be an adjustment all around.

I found myself daydreaming when I was by myself. I would take a pen and scribble "Becky Mason" on a piece of paper and then tear it to shreds. I wondered if Chance was going to ask me to marry him. Then I wondered what my answer would be if he did. Did I want to be a stepmother? I knew I loved Chance so I would push all these questions away and tell myself everything would work out the way it was supposed to. We had only been together a couple of months.

I would tell myself Chance's Mom and Dad fell in love at first sight so this could be true for us too. I finally realized that Chance was worth a shot even though I had kept him at arm's length for such a long time.

I was more nervous the first night we all stayed together than Cassidy was. She took it all in stride and acted like it was a sleepover. She wanted to go back to Chance's house too sometimes. It was almost like a game to her. Chance tucked her in and told her he would be back in a little while. We spent some quiet time talking and then went to bed. I remember wondering if I would be as accepting of this plan as his daughter was. Chance was certainly bending over backwards trying to please both of us. When I woke up the next morning and he was right beside me, I had a good feeling this was all going to work out.

Chapter 30

Everything was crazy busy at the recording studio as we worked on finishing the songs for the album. The photographer was working on the cover shots trying to make me look amazing. I told him he had his work cut out for him.

"No, I don't, Becky," he said. "You really are very photogenic."

I thanked him for the compliment. I was happy with the pictures, especially the way he focused on making the lighting very complimentary. I wore more makeup than usual, which made quite a difference. Everyone said how professional it looked. The album title was "Becky's World" and it showed me with all my cowgirl show stuff. I even bought a new hat.

Chance had Cassidy with him when he picked me up. He had asked Emily to have the cook at the dude ranch prepare us a nice dinner. I asked her to join us but she said she had a date with Ryan. After dinner, Cassidy seemed happy to go to Chance's parents' for the night. They were taking her to see "Frozen" and she was very excited. I was so used to him being in my life, I couldn't remember what life was like without him. Cassidy kept asking about her mother, however, and there wasn't much news to tell her. Chance called every day to see how she was doing.

Marty reminded me it was time to think again about going out on the road. He was looking at the venues and trying to decide which one would be best. I just wanted to stay home but I knew this wasn't an option. He said we would probably fly somewhere this time and I would be part of a big star's opening act. He was thinking about Jacksonville because it was a short flight from Nashville. Eric Church had a big show there at the amphitheater in a few weeks and he liked to have new artists as opening acts. Chance and I, along with Julie, Dixie and Marty would fly there. The rest of the crew would come by bus and we would all stay at the Hyatt Regency. Our first trip together! I was more excited to be going on a trip with Chance than I was about performing at the show. What on earth was going on with me?

Chapter 31

Chance just thought I was nervous and he was probably right. As the concert date approached, we rehearsed our one song a million times. We were doing an upbeat arrangement of one of the songs on the album. Marty thought SUPERSTAR was too melancholy for this crowd.

It seemed strange to board the flight as a regular passenger after riding free as an airline employee for so long. We arrived in Jacksonville in the morning and by the time we checked in at the hotel, we barely had time for lunch. Our equipment had arrived the night before and was already unloaded and set up. Kenny and the guys were doing a sound check when we arrived at the arena.

When I opened the door to my dressing room, Julie had my clothes all laid out and there was a huge bouquet of flowers on the table. The card read, "You'll knock 'em dead, Becky. Love, Chance" Now I let myself be excited.

There were three opening acts and I was the last one. The other two were male artists and they were very good. I was wishing I could have been first, to get it over with. When my name was called there was a lot of applause, which surprised me. I kissed Chance and walked up on stage like I had done so many times at home. No nerves, no butterflies, just a sense of complete happiness. We had rehearsed so many times I swear we could have performed it in our sleep. The crowd hooted and hollered when we all took a bow. It was over in a flash but I was still on a high when I walked into a bear hug from Chance. What a special moment.

People came over for autographs, which was something new and exciting. We all sat around in the bar and had a few drinks before watching Eric Church perform. This was my first big concert and I enjoyed every minute of it. I could hardly believe I was actually part of this musical experience.

After the concert was over, Chance and I went up to our room and had a drink by ourselves. I loved the way he looked at me when he knew we were going to make love. I knew he had been with other women but he made me feel like I was the only one who mattered.

Our first show had been everything I had ever dreamed of. Maybe it was the country rock music or just the experience of being part of a live show, but there was a closeness, an intimacy, we hadn't had before. We both said over and over how grateful we were that we found each other. I was constantly thanking the universe for sending me this wonderful man.

Chapter 32

We flew back home the next morning after meeting everyone for breakfast. Chance and I both couldn't wait to see Cassidy. She ran to her father and hugged him and then she ran to me, which choked me up a little. She was the sweetest thing.

Marty said the reviews for the show were through the roof. This was such good news especially with the album coming out in a couple months. He said I could stay home for a while and just sing at the local clubs in Nashville. I was very happy about this. He wanted me to promote SUPERSTAR as much as we could and hopefully get it into the country's top 40. Country radio was playing it regularly now too. Always without fail, the image of the military man would appear in my mind whenever I sang this song. I told Emily I thought I was losing it. She promised herself she would explain what was happening to me when we took our trip to Hilton Head.

Chance's dad told us there was going to be a big air show in Atlanta in a few months and he wanted to take all of us there to experience the excitement. We could stay overnight and fly back in the morning.

"What's the big deal?" I asked Chance. He said his dad was proud of this air demonstration team and wanted us to see it in person. I really had no interest but of course I would go along for the ride. Cassidy would probably love it too.

Chapter 33

The Country Music Awards were coming up at the Bridgestone Arena in Nashville the next month. For the last few years, I watched the show on TV from across the street in one of the bars while dreaming of being there myself. Marty said there was an outside possibility I could have a minute and a half wedged in between a TV commercial and an award presentation. Hey, I'd take what I could get. With any luck next year I could be nominated for new female artist of the year! Wouldn't that be something?

We decided to use SUPERSTAR for the one-minute spot. It would make an impression even if it was for a short time. Julie and I went shopping just in case. Everyone glammed up for this show. It was a very big deal. I found the perfect red dress and showed it to Chance to be sure. His eyes almost popped out of his head. I had never worn anything as revealing before.

The news about Carrie continued to be pretty much the same. She had a long way to go to be released from rehab. Cassidy sent her cards and told her she missed her. She was such a sensitive and loving child. Her birthday was coming up in a few days and Julie, Emily and I were planning a huge party for her. After all, being five was very special. She would be starting school in the fall. She was so excited about her party!

Her party was fun to plan. I ordered a cake with a pony and a little girl with five candles. Emily invited about twenty friends to a cookout. The dude ranch cook was preparing a big feast for everyone.

On the day of her party, one of the neighbors drove over and told Chance and me that one of their bitches had a litter of sheltie puppies about four months old and one of the boys had wandered off. They asked if we would keep an eye out for him. His name was Rusty. Cassidy overheard and went around to everyone at the party telling them little Rusty was lost and we had to find him.

Chance was happy to see his daughter so excited about her party. It was the first birthday he could spend with her. Everyone started to arrive around 4 pm. She ran up to everyone as they came in and squealed with delight as people gave her presents.

The guys had set up long tables out by the main pasture. When they brought the food out, Chance opened a couple of bottles of wine and put them on the table. He thanked us for putting this together. He held Cassidy on his lap until everyone had helped themselves to food and drinks. She wanted to get down and run around before Emily brought out the birthday cake.

It was a relaxed get together as everyone knew each other, some for a very long time. Everyone was remarking how cute Cassidy was and how darn smart she was too. Chance was very proud and you could tell how much he loved her.

Emily was poised to bring out the cake so Chance grabbed some matches to light the five candles. I turned around to see where Cassidy was but I couldn't see her. Emily stopped and waited with the cake.

"Chance!" I called out, "Where's Cassidy?" Chance spun around and searched the area with his eyes. "Where is she, Becky? I don't see her."

I looked over by the pasture and didn't see her there. Julie ran into the house to see if she had gone inside. She came out shaking her head. I could feel panic starting in my stomach. Chance and I called out to her, but she didn't answer. Within seconds, everyone started looking for her. Marty grabbed his phone and dialed the emergency Nashville police number. Two squad cars arrived within minutes. Chance called the child missing person number. The police had already alerted them. His face showed how upset he was. I tried to tell him she was probably hiding or something. He wasn't buying it.

Search teams were organized and started to comb through the pastures and woods. The police brought in a helicopter with searchlights. There was no sign of her. Chance ran over to the creek, which fortunately was low this time of year. I knew he was scared to death. Honestly, I was too.

Darkness was settling in but the searchers wouldn't quit. All of a sudden someone screamed, "We've got her!" Chance ran into the woods. I was right behind him. There she was, all cuddled up under a tree with the puppy. Chance picked her up and asked if she was all right.

"Yes, Daddy, but I couldn't leave little Rusty all alone out here."

He had tears of relief in his eyes as he carried her out of there. I took a breath for the first time in an hour and picked up the puppy. Word got around quickly she was found and safe. She asked if she could have her birthday cake now and open her presents. Chance told her we would have to do all of that tomorrow. Marty thanked the police and all the searchers with a megaphone we used to round up the horses. One by one everyone took off until just the family and close friends were left. Cassidy didn't understand why everyone was so upset. Chance was holding her like he was never going to let her go.

Chapter 34

Cassidy wanted to stay the night with us. She kept asking her father if he was mad at her. He explained why she could never wander away again. He didn't want to scare her and tell her there were bad people out there. So he just said we had to know where she was at all times.

When we were finally alone and Cassidy was asleep in her bed, I tried to soothe Chance and help him relax. He knew I was just as upset and scared as he was. We held each other until we fell asleep, thanking the universe for making everything right in our world.

The next morning the neighbor who owned the litter of puppies came over to thank Cassidy for finding Rusty and keeping him safe. She took Chance aside and asked if Cassidy could have him. They wanted her to have him as her very own puppy. Chance said yes, after he asked me if Rusty could stay here at the ranch with my shelties.

When we told Cassidy, you never saw a happier little girl. Those two must have bonded out in the woods and it was a beautiful sight. She had her birthday cake around lunchtime and finally opened her presents. Her biggest thrill, however, was having Rusty by her side. Again I saw myself in her when I was her age. I knew she would take wonderful care of him and my shelties were very happy to have a puppy to play with.

After all the drama and excitement, Chance and I just wanted to chill out for a day or two. It was so much fun to watch the older dogs teach the puppy the ropes. Rusty was very smart and caught on fast. Cassidy had already trained him to walk on a leash. Now, this is a picture: a little girl and a little puppy. Priceless.

Chance's mom and dad stopped over to see how things were going. They were out of town the night before and missed the search and all the excitement. Marty mentioned we should go to Hilton Head for a couple of days now that he bought a house. Chance had been there many times and told me how beautiful it was. His father had to apply for the free airline passes and would do this right away. We were lucky we could fly for free under Chance's father's flying privileges. They both said they would look after Cassidy and they would do fun things with her. I knew Emily and Julie would take care of the animals.

I asked Emily if she would mind if we postponed our trip to Hilton Head for a little while. Of course she understood and said we could go anytime. She was glad Chance and I were getting away for a couple of days.

There were so many plans to be made! We decided on the following week, which would give us time to coordinate everything. I hugged Chance and he was happy to see me so excited.

Chapter 35

We were going to stay in the house Marty bought which was on the ocean. I could hardly breathe I was so pumped up. We could walk to the beach club for dinner, which was close by. Chance knew all the places to go and everything there was to do. It would be very private when we wanted it to be.

I needed some new clothes of course so Julie and I took off for Nashville on a shopping spree. We were only going to be away for three days. Cowboy boots and western clothes were out. In with the bathing suits and shorts!

We spent the next week getting everything in place so we could leave on Monday. Because of the airline schedules, we had to fly from Nashville to Atlanta and change planes to get to Hilton Head Island. The week dragged by.

It was hard saying goodbye to everyone, especially Cassidy. Chance promised her we'd bring presents and do something really special when we got back. She seemed okay with us leaving and gave us special hugs. Chance's mom held her hand as we waved goodbye. She was a strong little kid. No tears. Can't say the same for Chance and me. As soon as we hit the highway I dried my tears, turned the radio way up and let myself get into the music. We were off on our big adventure.

The first leg was from Nashville to Atlanta. An hour later we were in Atlanta boarding our connecting flight. Within the hour we were landing on this beautiful island. Something about this seemed familiar. I must have seen a movie or something. The rental car was waiting for us and Chance knew exactly where we were going. I had never seen so many colorful flowers. It was beyond beautiful.

There were golf courses everywhere and all you could see was green grass, blue sky and clear water. We were staying on Sea Pines, one of the plantations with lots of golf courses. It was a gated community and we had to show ID to drive in. Chance had stayed in this same house before. Marty grabbed it when it went on sale a few months back. We drove into the driveway and parked. The ocean was 50 feet away. He grabbed our stuff and went inside. There was a huge living room and kitchen with two bedrooms and two baths upstairs. A huge deck faced the ocean. He opened a cabana and took out chairs and a table. I found the liquor cabinet and made us a drink. Life was good. There was something familiar about being here. Maybe Emily would tell me if we had stayed here before.

I wanted to sit and look at the ocean forever. It was so beautiful and I couldn't believe people actually lived here year round. We could see dolphins playing further out to sea. Boats went by and people waved. I couldn't recall a more idyllic time. Chance was so relaxed and happy too. He asked me if I was content being there with him. This was an understatement.

His father called to make sure we got there all right and had everything we needed. Cassidy wanted to say hi too. We missed her already.

After a while we decided to walk down to the beach club and have a drink. What a beautiful place. Ceiling to floor windows facing the ocean, with a bar cut through the length of the club. I knew exactly where I wanted to sit when we walked in. It was obvious to me even though I had no memory yet, that I had been there before.

Chapter 36

We had a lovely dinner at the club and slowly walked back arm in arm to the house. It must have been the ocean air because we both were suddenly exhausted.

Chance said laughing, "I never thought I'd say I was too tired to make love, but I think I am."

I smiled at him and said, "Don't bet on it," as I sat on the bed with him and started to undress. We both got our second wind in a hurry and fell asleep after a while, wrapped up together.

I whispered, "I love you," into his ear as I drifted off. We stirred on and off through the night unable to keep our hands off each other. It was a very romantic and loving time.

We woke up to the sun streaming through the windows and the sight and sound of the waves slowly touching the shore. Chance reached for me and we again made love. I couldn't get enough of him.

We had talked about taking the bikes out and touring the island. There were bike trails all over the place. I made coffee and we decided to have breakfast nearby at a small diner down the road. We both wanted some quiet time near the ocean and hoped we'd have time in the afternoon to just relax.

I looked over at this man who had become so important to me. I felt like we belonged together.

This trip was such a good idea and I was already wishing we had more time here. He sensed me watching him and walked over to kiss me.

"A penny for your thoughts, my dear," he smiled.

"How did I get so lucky?" I asked Chance.

He answered, "I'm the lucky one." He promised he would always appreciate what we have together and he would never take me for granted. "You are one in a million, Becky Steele and I love you."

I rested my head on his chest and said a thank you prayer to the universe for the love of this good man.

We took off on the bikes. It was a picture perfect day. I followed Chance because he knew where we were going. The trails weaved in and out of lagoons and private property. I screamed when I saw my first alligator sunning himself. We got off the bikes and walked on the sand down to the ocean. We took our shoes off and enjoyed walking in the salt water. We got back on the bikes and found our way to Harbour Town. Chance loved looking at all the boats and yachts. We had lunch in a small café filled with tourists with cameras. We met a nice couple from Nashville and exchanged personal information. They didn't recognize me because of my ball cap and sunglasses. I invited them to the ranch and to the Hummingbird. It's such a small world sometimes.

We rode our bikes back to the house, changed into bathing suits and walked down to the water's edge. I couldn't think of a better way to spend our day. I had remembered to pack extra suntan lotion, which we applied liberally to each other. The happiness we were feeling was beyond anything either one of us had ever experienced. We were deliriously in love.

Chapter 37

Chance woke me up gently the next morning. It would be our last full day on this spectacular island and he wanted it to be special. I was curious about what he was planning.

"What are you up to, Chance? You're very secretive about something." I knew he wasn't going to tell me but I kept trying to get it out of him. "You have to tell me sometime or I won't be a part of it."

He smiled and said, "You'll know soon enough."

Sure enough it wasn't long before a huge yacht appeared in the water out beyond our deck. A canoe with two men aboard came up onto the sand and waited until we got on board. I was surprised and had just enough time to grab some of my personal things. We had this private yacht for the whole day and night! There were personnel on board to take care of our every whim. Can you imagine? I couldn't wait to tell Emily. This must have cost a fortune!

There was a dolphin sighting scheduled for 10 am and we didn't want to miss it. This was something I had always wanted to do and I hoped we would see one or two up close. It turned out we saw a whole school of them and even had one come up to take food out of my hand. What a thrill this was. In a million years I never thought I'd be out in the middle of the Atlantic Ocean on a yacht no less. This was a once in a lifetime experience and I loved Chance for planning this for us.

We had lunch below deck and then were off to a secluded spot somewhere on the island. Our privacy was guaranteed and Chance made sure we had a few hours of quiet and alone time. There were chairs and lounges set up and even a stocked mini bar. Our host, Alex, had made sure everything was perfect. He took the canoe and paddled back out to the yacht leaving us completely alone. We had our phones in case we needed anything.

Chance put his arms around me. "Are you happy?"

I answered him with a smile and a hug. He led me over to a secluded area where there were blankets and towels on the beach. There was even a small restroom area nearby. Nothing was forgotten or left out. It was just the two of us making love on that beautiful beach. I never wanted to leave. It was heaven on earth being here alone with the man I loved.

We eventually had to get ready to go home. Chance took my hand and held me back.

"Wait a minute, not yet."

I couldn't imagine what else he was thinking about. He handed me a vodka and tonic and said, "One more for the road." We toasted each other and promised we'd come back someday soon. I picked up my glass to take a drink and saw a flash of light or something shiny in the glass.

I put it down and said "What the..."

Chance was smiling from ear to ear. I reached into the bottom of the glass and pulled out the most beautiful diamond ring I had ever seen. Tears filled my eyes as I realized what this meant. Chance got down on one knee and told me how much he loved me and how he wanted to spend the rest of his life with me by his side.

"Will you marry me Becky? And Cassidy would be so happy too."

"Yes, yes, yes, of course, yes. I love you to the moon and back."

I leaned into him and put my arms around him. I could feel the love energy between us pulsing back and forth. I felt completely safe and protected with his arms around me. How I wished this moment could last forever.

Alex arrived to take us back to the yacht and wanted to know why I was crying. I showed him my hand.

"Wow, good taste, man," he said," It's beautiful."

I was so overcome with emotion I hadn't even really looked at the ring, a beautiful solitaire diamond with tiny accent diamonds on either side. The band was gold. I absolutely loved it. How did he know what size? Emily must have had a hand in this.

Meanwhile back home Emily and Julie were enlisting the men's help in hanging a "CONGRATULATIONS BECKY AND CHANCE!" banner across the front porch. I guess they knew I would say yes. Cassidy was jumping up and down and hugging everyone, she was so happy.

Chapter 38

Emily had called our family and a few of our friends to greet us at the ranch when we arrived. Everyone crowded around trying to see my ring. With all the hugs and congratulations floating around, there was no time to tell Emily any of the details of our trip. I told her I wouldn't leave anything out when we had a chance to talk.

Cassidy went flying into her father's arms when she saw him.

"Daddy, daddy, are you going to marry Becky? Is she going to be my stepmother? Her little face shone with excitement and happiness.

I hugged her and told her I loved her daddy and I loved her too. We had bought her a couple of surprises at Harbour Town and she said it felt like Christmas. One was a stuffed dolphin, which she carried around all day. She named him Smiley. I wanted so much to be the kind of mother to her that my mother was to me.

The guys were teasing Chance, saying something like "Boy, you didn't waste any time," along with all the hand shaking and congratulations. Everyone was so happy for us. I think Marty knew in the back of his mind this would happen but maybe not quite so soon.

Chance took Cassidy over to see his parents. His mother wasn't feeling well, so she didn't come to the ranch. This gave Emily and me some time alone. I wanted to tell her how the beach club in Hilton Head seemed so familiar. I recognized the house and remembered she and I had stayed there before. I told her all about our romantic times and how wonderful and loving Chance was. She was really happy for us.

"When are you getting married?" she asked.

I told her we hadn't even thought about it. I noticed she looked like she didn't feel well and I hoped she wasn't catching a bug or something.

Marty wanted to take us out to dinner to celebrate so we took a shower and changed our clothes. I hadn't seen Dixie yet because she was working but we knew we would see her at dinner. I wondered if and when Chance would tell Carrie. As far as we knew she was still in rehab. She would certainly not be happy that we were engaged.

When we finally did see Dixie, she hugged us for ten minutes. She was so happy because she knew that Chance would always take care of me. She was becoming more and more like my second mom. There was such a loving way about her and reminded me of my own mother in so many ways. Even though she loved to cook, she had managed to keep her weight in check and was still a very attractive woman. Everyone was having fun talking at once over dinner. It's a wonderful thing to be surrounded by people who love you. Cassidy still had her dolphin and wouldn't let it go. We had a wonderful time celebrating our engagement. We were getting married! I kept pinching myself to prove it wasn't a dream.

We were exhausted from all the excitement and traveling. After we said goodnight to everyone,

—

we took Cassidy and went home. She laid down on our bed with us and we all fell asleep in the blink of an eye.

Chapter 39

My phone started ringing first thing in the morning. I rolled over and looked at Chance who was barely awake. Cassidy woke up and Chance carried her over to her room. I grabbed the phone to stop it from ringing. A distraught Sue Ellen from the dude ranch was trying to tell me that Emily had called in sick.

I said, "What? She never calls in sick."

Sue Ellen said she had a handle on everything but she had never been alone on the job before and she was nervous.

"I'm sure you'll be fine, "I told her. "I'll go check on Emily. Call me back if there's a problem."

I knocked on Emily's bedroom door. She answered, looking like death warmed over.

"What's going on Em? Are you ok? You never blow off work." She told me to sit down on the bed and close the door.

"I'm late," she whispered.

"Late for what?" I replied.

She gave me a look.

I sat up straight. "How late?"

"About two months."

My mind went backwards to the night I saw her walking up to the bunkhouse with Ryan.

"You didn't use anything? Are you crazy?"

She said she never missed her pill so she didn't understand how this could happen. Yup, they say 98 percent effective. It's the two percent that gets you.

I got up to leave and she asked me where I was going. I told her the drugstore was five minutes away and I was going to pick up a pregnancy test.

"I'll be right back. Eat some crackers or something."

I was back in 10 minutes. She was afraid to take the test but I told her she had to.

"We have to know what we're dealing with. Take it." She came out of the bathroom with a look of complete despair on her face.

"It's positive. I'm pregnant."

I hugged her and told her everything would work out.

"You need to tell your parents and you also need to tell Ryan. Was this a one night stand or what?" I asked. "Do you even like him?"

She didn't answer, just said her head was reeling but she needed to go to work now that she felt better. She would think about everything else later. I left her alone to get dressed.

What would she do? I thanked God this didn't happen to me. It just as easily could have.

Chance was still in bed. I crawled in next to him and snuggled into his arms. He asked me about Emily. I told him there was a problem.

He said, "Oh no..." like he knew what it was.

"Who has she been messing around with?"

"Ryan."

He shook his head. "Not a long term prospect. I hope she's not in love with him."

I told him I thought it was just a one-night thing and they got caught. "She's back at work, feeling better. You know if there is a baby, there are enough people around here to help her. It could be a lot worse."

Cassidy heard us talking and knocked on the door. Chance yelled, "Come in," and she ran through the door and jumped up on the bed with us. What a happy little girl she was!

Emily caught up with me later in the day. She asked for some time off so she could talk to Ryan.

"Sure," I replied." Whatever you need."

She climbed into the food truck with Ryan when he was feeding the horses. I saw the truck parked by the side of the road.

After a while, they came back and Emily walked over to me as I was brushing Skipper. I asked her how it went and she said he was shocked because we were so careful. He agreed he would support her in every way but there were no feelings between them so she was pretty much on her own. Next she had to tell her parents.

Her mom and dad were upset of course, but they told her they would stand by her and were glad she was going to keep the baby. She made a doctor's appointment for the next week and I told her I would go with her. The morning sickness had let up some so she was able to work and carry on with her life. Everyone agreed to keep this private for now so there wouldn't be a lot of gossip. It was really nobody's business. Ryan was concerned about his job and Marty told him there was no problem with him continuing to work at the ranch as long as there were no friction problems between him and Emily.

Chapter 40
BRANSON MISSOURI

Justin Roe turned the radio in his red pick up truck up high. Country radio was playing my new single and talking about my being an aspiring young artist. He was listening to SUPERSTAR. He was planning on going to the CMA awards in Nashville next month and he wondered how he could arrange a meeting with me. He had seen my picture online. He made a note to remind himself to ask his manager if he could set this up.

Justin was on leave from his tour with the Silver Eagles air demonstration team and was planning on moving to Nashville as soon as his commitment to the Eagles was over in the next three months. I had always said how handsome these men were and Justin was no exception. He had blue eyes that looked right through you. He wanted a record contract more than anything and realized you could only go so far in the music business in Branson. His manager thought it was time to try his luck with the big boys in Nashville.

He had done his research. He knew my manager owned The Hummingbird Café in Nashville and he wanted to audition there on open mic night. He thought knowing me might help him get an audition.

Back in Franklin, Chance and I were having dinner at The Trick Pony on our first date as an engaged couple. We were sitting on the same side in the booth and he had his arm around me.

"So when should we get married, Miss Steele, any ideas?"

I almost choked on my salad and asked why he was in such a big hurry. We spent almost all our free time together now anyway. Chance kissed me on the cheek and said he couldn't wait until I was his wife. This handsome hunk was just the sweetest guy.

Cassidy wasn't with us because she had a play date with one of our guests who had a daughter her age. They were watching a movie together on a big screen in the living room at the dude ranch. I asked Chance if he missed her. He said he did but it was nice just having time for the two of us. The CMA awards were fast approaching and he knew how crazy things would be before long.

I looked up and saw Marty and Dixie coming in the door. I waved them over to sit with us. Marty said he wanted to talk to me about something so it was a nice coincidence they found us. I didn't believe in coincidences so I wondered what this was about. Chance got up to get us a drink and Dixie, with a new spiffy haircut, went to say hello to a friend a couple tables away.

Marty said he had received a phone call from the producer of Big Dream Branson about a young artist relocating to Nashville. His name was Justin Roe and he was a big fan of mine. I said I didn't think I had been around long enough to have any big fans. Marty said he wanted to meet me and maybe we could all have a drink after the CMA's.

I said "Sure, as long as he knows I'm engaged and all."

I thought this was kind of strange but then forgot about it when Marty and Dixie sat down with us to have dinner. I made a point to compliment Dixie on her new look. Marty said she looked twenty again. So much for our alone time.

Chapter 41

The CMA's were fast approaching. I had gotten a one-minute spot and knew I had to make the most of it. Millions of people would be watching on TV so the publicity was invaluable. All the participants were allowed to come into the Bridgestone Arena and get a feel for the stage areas. I wanted to be sure I wouldn't get dizzy on the turning stage in my 90 seconds of fame. Chance the fiancé became Chance the bodyguard and couldn't sit with us. He had to stand so he could watch what was going on around us. Fans at the CMA awards get crazy sometimes.

Meanwhile Emily and I went to her doctor's appointment. The doctor said she was healthy and prescribed some prenatal vitamins. Emily had a resigned attitude about the pregnancy. She wasn't really happy or sad, just accepting of the fact that there was going to be a baby in about six months. I insisted she go to the CMA awards show with us. She wasn't showing yet and she had bought a new green dress to wear. I thought it would be good for her to dress up and go out to the big show. Plus, I could use all the support I could get. I had always known a person's life can change in an instant. Well, Emily's was about to change for the second time.

Chance kept telling me to calm down. I was pretty nervous about performing at the CMA's. I had rehearsed with the band there so I was ready. It was just the idea of it, all those people staring at me. I was almost wishing I didn't have to do it. Marty told me to just sing like I always did and it would be over before I even knew it. He was right. It took longer to walk up the stairs than it did to sing a few bars of SUPERSTAR. Whew. I was so glad when it was over. I'm glad I did it.

Chance and Emily were very supportive and I was happy they were there. We headed for the bar area where Marty said the singer from Branson was waiting. I had forgotten all about him and explained to Chance that the guy was just a fan.

Justin Roe introduced himself to Marty and then Marty introduced him to all of us. I noticed Emily perk up when she saw him. He shook my hand and said how happy he was to meet me. I introduced him to Chance and they shook hands too. Marty bought us all a round of drinks and started to tell Justin about The Hummingbird and open mic night. I asked Justin if he'd be in town for a couple of days so we could show him the ropes. He said he'd be around and would meet us at The Hummingbird on Wednesday night.

Emily had walked over and started to talk to him about his career and what he was looking for. They seemed to be getting along well after just meeting each other. There was something vaguely familiar about him, but I didn't say anything to anyone. He told Emily about his father playing SUPERSTAR over and over when he lived at home. She didn't get the connection right away because Justin's last name was Roe, shortened from

"Munroe." I didn't understand at the time either but this man was my ex-boyfriend Johnny's son.

We all had another round of drinks and decided to head home. Emily said she was going to stay awhile and Justin would drive her home.

I kiddingly said, "Don't be late for work in the morning."

She smiled and told me not to worry.

Chance shook Justin's hand and told him he'd see him Wednesday. As we were getting in the truck, I asked him what he thought about this new guy. Chance just shrugged and said, "Emily likes him. He seems okay to me." I had stared at Justin trying to figure out where I had seen him before.

"Maybe when I see him sing Wednesday, I'll remember," I said to myself.

Chapter 42

Emily must have been up all night because she made coffee at the crack of dawn. I heard her in the kitchen so I got up very quietly. She couldn't wait to tell me about this new guy.

"Becky, Becky, I like this Justin. I can hardly wait to hear him sing."

I asked her if anything happened between them. She said no, he was a perfect gentleman. She said they were going out for coffee later and she was going to show him where The Hummingbird Café was. I asked her if she was going to tell him she was pregnant. She said absolutely not. There was no reason to, at least not yet. I was shaking my head a little over this but it was really none of my business.

Chance heard us talking and came into the kitchen to have coffee. Cassidy was with his parents and it seemed strange not to have her there.

"What are you girls whispering about at 6 am?" he laughed.

I told him we were talking about men. What else?

Emily grabbed her coffee and ran out the door heading over to the dude ranch.

"Have a good day," she called over her shoulder.

Chance and I looked at each other and raced back to the bedroom. After we'd made love, Chance turned serious and told me he had to talk to me about something. He said he had been trying hard to find the right time.

"What's wrong?" I asked. I was very concerned and a little scared.

"Nothing's wrong," he answered as he put his arms around me. "There's something about me you need to know that's all."

I sat up in bed. "This sounds serious."

He said it was but it was nothing to be worried about. He wanted to wait to tell me until he was sure we had a future together. He told me that after he graduated from college up north he applied to the New York State Police for a position as a state trooper. He was accepted and spent some time at the State Police Academy in Albany. He loved his job and was promoted to an undercover agent in no time. When his parents decided to move to Tennessee, he was torn about whether he should go with them. He flew down to Nashville and made an appointment with the attorney general to see if his experience and background could be useful to his department. He was offered a job as a special investigator on the spot. This is not public knowledge and he was asked to only tell those closest to him.

I asked who knew about this here in Nashville. He answered no one but me but he needed to tell Marty. I thought back to when Cassidy disappeared and how he knew the right people to call. He told me I could tell Emily but only if she swore not to tell anyone. I told him I was proud of him and this made him even sexier, if that were possible. We both laughed.

He got dressed and headed up to the main house to talk to Marty. When I saw him later, he told me Marty had a feeling he was trained in police work. That's why he asked him to look out for me on the road.

Chapter 43

This had turned into quite an event, going to The Hummingbird to see this cowboy from Branson. Emily was bubbling all over the place with excitement and it seemed to be contagious. Even Marty and Dixie were excited. Mr Barkley from Dream Big Nashville was coming too. I hoped this guy would be good enough for all the attention. Chance picked me up and we followed Justin and Emily into the parking lot.

When we arrived The Hummingbird was packed. It usually was on open mic night, but this was even more so. All the tables were full and there were people standing in the back. Marty had reserved us a table up front. Justin was in a good mood and didn't seem nervous at all. He had a nice way about him and I could see why Emily liked him so much. After a few regulars sang their songs, Marty introduced Justin to the crowd. There was a lot of applause. My three backup musicians were on stage with him. They had rehearsed a little in the afternoon. Kenny had called me and said, "This guy is good. Wait till you hear him."

He chose a popular upbeat Kenny Chesney tune which was one of my favorites. Emily and I made eye contact almost as soon as he opened his mouth. This guy was good, really good, and I could see the dollar signs in Marty's eyes. Justin took off his hat and waved to the crowd, which was literally going nuts. It looked like Mr. Barkley and Marty had made a decision before Justin even sat back down. Emily was beaming. I had to admit there was something special about him and I just knew he was going to be a big star.

Marty, the producer, and Justin Roe huddled at a table while the rest of the wannabe singers did their thing. I felt sorry for them because Justin had stolen the spotlight. Chance told me it was much like the first night I sang on the same stage.

He said, "Everyone knew you were a winner then too." I had no idea Chance had seen me back then.

After the powwow and the hand shaking, Justin came back to our table and we all congratulated him. There was nothing phony about him. He thanked me for giving him this opportunity and said he couldn't wait to choose his music. We all had a drink and toasted to his success.

Chance and I got up to leave and we said goodnight to everyone. I could see the looks between Justin and Emily and knew the sparks were flying. I wondered how Emily would handle this. I would be sure to talk to her about it in the morning. She didn't seem to mind that she was old enough to be his mother. Chance just told me to mind my own business.

Chapter 44

The siren from the ambulance cut through the quiet night like a knife. Chance and I heard it and woke up at the same time. It sounded close, really close. Chance threw some clothes on and ran outside. The lights were coming on around the ranch. What had happened? It didn't seem like a car accident or a fire. Cassidy was at Chance's parents so we knew she was safe. The ambulance had pulled up and parked in front of the dude ranch with the lights on but the siren off. Chance motioned to me to follow him. Marty and Dixie had come outside. The EMTs were bringing someone out on a stretcher. I ran over to the police officer and I told him I had to know who it was. He said it was someone who worked there. I ran over to the stretcher.

Emily saw me coming and cried out, "Becky, Becky!"

I ran to her side. "What happened?"

She started to cry, "I lost the baby, I lost the baby," she sobbed. She said she tripped inside on the steps and fell. She had called 911 from her phone.

They were taking her to the hospital so I told Emily that Chance and I would follow. "I'll be right behind you, don't be scared," I told her.

Chance picked me up in his truck.

"Please," I told him. "I have to go to the hospital with her." He said he'd take me.

I had the presence of mind to call her parents in Nashville. They met the ambulance at the hospital.

When we got there, Emily had been admitted to be sure she was all right. She was distraught. She said Justin had taken her to the dude ranch but didn't come in with her. "If he had come in, maybe I wouldn't have fallen." I told her this wasn't her fault. It was just a terrible accident. She said she should have gone home instead of trying to get a head start for the morning. I climbed up on the bed with her and held her while she cried. Chance left us alone.

Soon her parents came in and sat with us for a few minutes and then went to their house to wait for her. The nurse came in after a while and said she could go home as soon as the doctor checked her over. He came right along and did the paperwork so she could be discharged. Chance took her out to the truck in a wheelchair and I climbed into the back seat. I called her mom to tell her we were on the way to their house. I was trying hard not to cry.

Her mom met us at the house and took her inside. I hugged her and told her to take all the time she needed before she came back to work. I told her to call me anytime. Chance took me back to the ranch and sat with me in the truck for a long time. I just needed to hold his hand. The staff, without knowing what was going on, had all stepped up and covered for Emily. What a great bunch of people worked here. They told me not to worry. They would cover for her until she came back to work.

—

I wondered if Ryan knew and Chance said he would go find him and tell him. I kissed him and got out of the truck. I needed to go take a shower and start my day.

Emily reached out to me a lot during the next few weeks. She was grieving and needed my help getting through the pain. There wasn't much I could do except to be there with her.

I asked her about Justin and she said they decided to just be friends. Then one day out of the blue she called him at his hotel and asked him to go out to dinner with her. He was glad she called because he was going back to Branson in a few days to pack up his stuff and have it shipped to Nashville. He needed a place to live, so this was his first priority. I mentioned the trailer out by the bunkhouse if he wanted to stay there until he found something. Emily said she would tell him. They had a nice dinner at The Trick Pony and he said he'd get in touch when he came back. She was starting to be herself again. I mentioned the twenty-year age difference between them.

Emily laughed and said, "If it doesn't bother him, it doesn't bother me." I had to admit she looked like a teenager.

For the time being, business at the ranch had slowed down a little and Emily and I decided to go out to lunch. There was so much to talk about. Before I told her what happened at Hilton Head, I told her I had a secret to tell her about Chance. She had to promise on a stack of bibles not to tell anyone, not even Justin. She promised and I told her this was very serious. She had to keep this secret. Again she promised and I could tell she was dying to know what it was.

Her eyes got wider and wider as I explained Chance's job as a special investigator. She was impressed and said she always felt safe when he was around. I told her I felt the same way.

Then we talked about the weird things that happened at Hilton Head. She listened as I told her about the Beach Club and the house she and I had stayed in. I mentioned SUPERSTAR and told her about the man's face appearing in my mind. There were so many things. She didn't speak for a few minutes as if she was taking it all in. When she was ready, she replied.

"Becky, I understand everything you're saying. You see, the things you remember I remember too because I was there. Your memory is coming back and if you have any questions, just ask me."

I sat there stunned. Of course, Emily didn't lose her memory like I did. I told her we needed to take a trip over to Hilton Head sooner than later, or at least go somewhere private and talk.

Emily also realized Justin remembering hearing his father playing SUPERSTAR over and over meant something really big. She told Justin she had figured out that his father was Johnny Munroe. She also knew that since the accident I had no memory of the man I fell in love with so many years ago. So for now she decided not to say anything and see what happened at the air show if Johnny was there. She also thought of Chance. He wouldn't be very happy if an old boyfriend of Becky's surfaced out of nowhere.

Chapter 45

Somehow in between everything else going on, we managed to work on and record the next five songs for the debut album. The release date was about a month away. The name of the album was, "Becky Loves Tennessee," and it featured a really good picture of the ranch with me standing with Skipper and my pink guitar. I looked like a real cowgirl, complete with chaps.

Chance reminded me about the big air show in Atlanta coming up soon. His father was still insisting we all go and have a good time. I wondered if Justin would be there even though he was on leave. Maybe he could get us better seats or something. It was not something I was looking forward to. Emily said she'd find out the next time she talked to him.

Ultimately Justin returned from Branson and moved into the small trailer near the bunkhouse. He needed to find something bigger but for now it would have to do. He asked Marty if he could set up another trailer there and pay rent for the land. He liked being so close to all of us especially to Emily.

She asked him about the air show and he said he would be there as a spectator. He didn't realize Chance's father was retired Air Force. He told Emily the show was really exciting to watch and there would be thousands of people there.

He proudly stated, "My father served two years as an Eagle and was instrumental in encouraging me to join."

Emily was excited about going to the show even though it certainly wasn't her first time. She had hung out with me for a lot of the shows we went to so long ago. Unbeknownst to me, Emily was also intrigued by the unknown dynamics of Johnny and Justin and my amnesia, which was clearing little by little.

Justin mentioned that he was going to Georgia in a day or two to see his father. He knew he would be busy working and recording and didn't know when he would get another chance to go. When he told Emily, she smiled to herself and knew right where he was going. She remembered the diner where she and Becky, in disguise, had had peach pie where they last saw Johnny and his handsome son Justin.

Chance's mom had reserved a floor in the hotel in Atlanta for all of us. This way we would be all together. I wondered if Justin and Emily would be sharing a room. Once again, Chance told me it was none of my business.

Chapter 46
PERRY GEORGIA

Justin got off the plane in Atlanta and shook his father's hand. They were very close and didn't get to see each other very often. Justin hadn't yet told him he had moved to Franklin, Tennessee and was living at The Hummingbird Ranch. He also had not mentioned the recording contract or that he saw Becky and Emily every day. He just didn't know where to start.

The first thing he wanted to do when he got to Georgia was go to Mama's Diner for some peach pie. At the diner, Johnny could tell there was something on his son's mind. Justin said he had a lot to tell him. When he mentioned Becky he said she had a big cowboy for a boyfriend. Johnny sat there with his eyes wide as can be as Justin filled him in. Johnny was thrilled about his son's record deal and happy for Justin who seemed to have found his place in the recording industry in record time.

"There's more Dad," Justin said. "Emily and I are seeing each other and I think it's getting serious." Johnny told him Emily was a great girl and he thought very highly of her. "We had a lot of fun in the Silver Eagles days. Obviously the age difference doesn't bother you."

Justin thought he should tell his father about Becky's accident and how she doesn't remember anything about him. When he heard the news, Johnny said he was sorry to hear this but that it really didn't matter any more. Soon there was a second piece of pie. Justin mentioned the Atlanta air show and told his father they were all going.

Johnny said, "Wow this should be interesting. I wonder if Mike is going."

Justin shook his head and said to himself, "This is going to be a disaster if both these men see Becky at the same time. "They left the diner and went to Johnny's house on the lake and hung out on the boat for the rest of the day.

Justin's flight back to Nashville was at noon the next day. Emily met him at the airport. "All hell is going to let loose at the air show," he said to her.

She wanted to know what he was talking about and he tried to tell her on the way back to the ranch. Emily realized she better tell me what I had forgotten about Johnny and Mike. She needed to get me alone, away from Chance and Cassidy. After all, we might not be able to get to Hilton Head before the show.

A couple mornings later I was outside with my horses when I saw Justin leave the trailer and walk towards me. He definitely reminded me of someone. I called out "good morning" and stopped what I was doing. I wanted to talk to him privately about how he knew my name and about SUPERSTAR. We walked over to the side of the pasture and sat on a bench. He was very easy to talk to and very down to earth. He explained that his father knew the song and would play it on his CD player over and over. He remembered his father talking about a "Becky" he used to know. He said he would find a picture and bring it to me. I tried to explain there were a lot of years I didn't remember because of my fall. Emily saw us and wandered over. I got up and went back to working with my horses after I thanked Justin for talking with me. I told Emily about Justin's father playing SUPERSTAR over and over. Emily knew it was Johnny but kept it to herself.

Chapter 47

The air show was the next night. Early in the morning our flight was to leave for Atlanta. Cassidy decided not to go and then at the last minute changed her mind. Chance's mom said she'd watch her and she could stay in their hotel room. We were up and out of the ranch at the crack of dawn. I really wanted to stay in bed and I knew I'd be tired all day from getting up so early. We all got to the airport somehow and were on board the plane a half hour before departure. It was a short flight to Atlanta.

We all checked into our rooms and Chance and I took a nap. The show wasn't until 1 pm so we had plenty of time. The weather was good and the sky was clear. It was a perfect day for an air show. Justin took charge along with Chance's dad and told us where to meet at noon. There were a million cars but we had a car-parking pass to get up front. I looked at the pass and vaguely remembered it. I said to myself, "Oh no, I hope this doesn't go on all day." I had no idea my memories were starting to re-emerge.

We parked the car inside the gates and started to walk up closer to the runway. The pilots were outside of their planes signing autographs. I stopped walking and stared. I recognized the blue jumpsuits. I recognized the red white and blue jets with the eagle on the door. I recognized everything, the way the planes were lined up, the concession stands and the public announcement trailer. I grabbed Emily.

"It's happening again." It was like I was there, in another time, another place. My memories were coming back.

We had to go back to our seats, as the show was about to start. The bleachers were packed. The jets took off and proceeded to dazzle the big crowd with all kinds of formations and aerobatics. It was surprisingly exciting to watch. The applause from the crowd was deafening. I knew I had seen it all before.

I noticed Emily staring at someone. I followed her gaze and saw Justin with another man. For a minute I thought I knew him. The goosebumps were on high alert. I just didn't understand why.

Justin walked over to me when it was over and asked how I liked the show. I told him, "I swear I remember seeing this air show many times."

Justin just said, "Well, maybe you did."

I didn't notice the handsome man in sunglasses walking back and forth in front of us.

After the show we got into the pizza line. Chance put Cassidy up on his shoulders so she wouldn't get trampled with all the people. I tried to get everyone together so we could arrive at the airport on time. We just made it. We were back in Nashville in a couple of hours. Emily told me she'd see me in the morning. We all agreed the show was amazing. Cassidy said she liked the show but it was too loud. Chance let his mom take her for the night and he and I went to bed early. Emily was at the trailer with Justin and didn't come home that night.

Chapter 48

Emily made coffee early the next morning and included a cup for Chance.

"Becky, we have to talk," she said urgently.

Justin knocked on the door with a coffee cup in one hand and an envelope in the other. Chance opened the door and let him in. He kissed Emily on the cheek as he walked by. Her green eyes sparkled as she looked at him.

"Did you bring the picture?" I asked.

He said, "Yes, this is a picture of my father in his Silver Eagles uniform. It was taken a few years ago." Emily told Justin not to give me the picture yet. Whoops, too late. He took the 5 x 7 photograph out of the envelope and handed it to me. I was afraid to look at it but everyone was staring at me, so I had to. I gasped when I realized it was the man I saw in my mind whenever I sang SUPERSTAR.

"It's him. I'm sure of it. What is his name?"

Bells and whistles went off in my head when Justin answered, "Johnny Munroe."

I saw images in my head of this man with me, in my car, in restaurants, at air shows, in motel rooms, in my bed. Emily tried to tell me to calm down. She turned to Justin.

"Damn, Justin, I wanted to tell her before she saw the picture."

Justin's face was white as a sheet. Chance didn't know what to think. He didn't have a clue what was going on with me.

Emily asked Justin and Chance to leave us alone. I was trying to calm down and listen to her. She very calmly and with every detail she could think of described how I met Johnny and fell in love with him. She told me how I traveled to meet him every chance I got. She explained how these men had girlfriends that they called "holecards" when they were on the road going to air shows. I asked her if he loved me. She said there were times when he acted like he did but would make no commitment to me and wouldn't see me after the show season ended.

"So, basically he was using me?" My voice took on a mind of its own.

Emily said, "No, not really. It was just the way things were on the road."

I shook my head. "I was a groupie? How could I do that, Emily?"

She answered, "You loved him and nothing I could say would sway you from the way you felt about him."

I was in shock and found it difficult to believe her. The fact remained however, I had been nothing more than a doormat. I was gradually starting to remember him.

I wanted to know if she talked to him at the show.

She said, "For a minute when you were getting pizza. He wanted to talk to you but I told him no way. I should have told you sooner. I'm sorry."

As more and more pieces of the memories came into my conscious mind, I found myself straining to remember as much as I could. For instance, I could vividly remember some of the love scenes one moment and then there would be nothing, just a blank. One thing was clear to me, though, I had been deeply in love with this man.

Emily was fascinated and wanted to know everything even though she remembered a lot of it. I told her whatever I could remember, like when I saw American Idol on TV and heard SUPERSTAR for the first time. Then there was the time she and I put on wigs and went searching for Johnny all over Georgia.

Like I always say, you can't make this stuff up. Emily was with me for all of it.

Meanwhile, Emily was falling hard for Justin. It was nice to see her in love with a kind, decent man. She had a constant smile on her face and I loved seeing her so happy. The age difference didn't mean a thing. They went everywhere together and Emily totally supported his singing career. Marty mentioned there should be a duet recorded with Justin and me one of these days. He thought Justin was the next Kenny Chesney.

I had Justin make a copy of his father's picture for me. I hid it in a drawer so Chance wouldn't see it. I wanted to be able to look at the man I was once so in love with and see if the picture would bring back any more memories.

Chapter 49

Justin had gone back to his trailer and Chance was wearing a groove outside the door in the dirt from pacing. Emily went to work and I opened the door to let Chance back in. He wanted to know what the hell happened. I tried to explain that I just found out Justin's father was an old boyfriend of mine. I was just starting to remember him. He was one of the Silver Eagles and was at the air show. Chance asked me if I saw him and talked to him.

I honestly said, "No, Emily said he wanted to talk to me but she kept him away."

Chance wanted to know if we had been serious. How do you tell the man you love, who respects you, that you followed this guy around like a dog and thought you loved him? I honestly told him I thought we were but that I had been too young to understand what was going on. Chance said he saw these women at the rodeos and at concerts. The air show was a new one on him.

He put his arm around me and said, "We both have pasts. I don't judge you anymore than you've judged me. It's ok, Becky, what's done is done."

I put my arms around him and told him how much I loved him. I decided to take a day off and stay right there with him and make him understand how much I had changed and grown up.

I curled up with Chance and tried to sleep. He was so sweet and didn't ask any questions or try to get me to talk. He called over to the dude ranch to get some food brought over. I was surprised I was so hungry. After I ate a sandwich I actually felt better.

Justin caught up with me the next day at The Hummingbird. He had called his father and told him about my accident and my memory loss. It was a hard one to believe all right. I promised Justin I'd sing SUPERSTAR that night at The Hummingbird so I'd be able to tell if there were going to be any more memory images.

His father wanted to come and see me sometime. Honestly, that would be kind of weird and I didn't know if I could manage it. I wondered why Justin's last name was different. He explained he dropped the "Mun" from Munroe because he thought Justin Roe sounded better.

I was shocked at the number of cars in the parking lot. There was a full house with standing room only at The Hummingbird. Chance was busy keeping fans away from our table. After the first time we sang SUPERSTAR, we had to sing it again because there were so many requests. There were no memory images or interruptions of any kind for me. For the first time there were no tears. I took a deep breath and told myself the nightmare was over. No goosebumps either, all was quiet.

A few days later, Justin knocked at the door and wanted to talk. Chance was working at the rodeo for the weekend and Emily had to take her mom somewhere. I welcomed him in and put on a pot of coffee. He said he wanted to give me a few days to let the dust settle before we talked about everything that happened.

"Becky, you really are starting to remember my father?" He asked as if it couldn't be true.

"I remember some things, yes, Justin. I remember how much I loved him."

Justin answered, "Wow, Becky, my dad is never going to believe this. He wants to come here and see you. Would you be willing to spend some time with him?"

I hesitated for a moment, and told him it would not be a good idea. In the back of my mind I was thinking this absolutely was NOT a good idea.

I changed the subject. There was a lot of publicity surrounding the album release so I told Justin I had to go down to The Hummingbird for pictures and autographs. He was welcome to come if he wanted to. After all, he was going to be doing the same thing soon.

He said, "Hell yeah," and went over to the trailer to get his truck. I texted Chance and Emily and told them we'd be back in a couple of hours. Marty was glad to see Justin and introduced him around. There were a lot of people there and the track from my new album was playing in the background. It looked like it was going to be a huge success. Mr. Barkley was there from the label but instead of talking to me, he wanted to know if Justin was ready to sign a contract. Marty and I encouraged him and he signed on the dotted line. I texted Emily and sent a picture. This was a big moment for him. His dad will be so proud.

Marty then told us to get our butts down there and work on a duet. They would include it in Justin's album. We set something up for the next day. Justin practically flew back to the ranch he was so excited. I think Marty was right. He was going to be great.

Marty took the time to explain the changes in the music business. In a few years there would be no record stores and music would be streamed on computers and phones. It may very well be the CD's and albums we were making would be obsolete soon. Artists would still be paid of course but it would be on a different scale. He also said the covers would be collectors' items some day.

Chapter 50

Emily was beyond excited for Justin and so was I. We all went down to The Hummingbird in the late morning the next day. My guys were all set up and waiting. Marty and Mr. Barkley were there too. I was glad he chose a song I knew. I told him to just sing like he was by himself and I would come in with the harmony when I could. I told him we might have to practice a few times. Singing harmony was not my thing.

Everyone was amazed at how well our voices meshed. He was so handsome you just wanted to hug him. I could see why Emily was smitten.

After a couple tries, we were ready. They turned the recording equipment on and we gave it a shot. When it was over, everyone applauded and we waited for the test so we could hear it. I was shocked at how good it was.

Marty kept saying, "I told you, I told you."
I was very proud of Justin and so happy that he didn't let his nerves affect the music. I know I keep saying it. He was going to be a star.

Chapter 51

The CMA awards were the next week at the Bridgestone Arena in Nashville. Marty pulled some strings and got good seats for us. I knew the TV cameras would be all over the place and that I would have to smile a lot. I counted eleven of us if I didn't forget anyone. Cassidy had a new sparkly dress and a tiara for her hair. Justin was so excited to go and get a chance to see all the famous people in person.

This was a very big deal. I couldn't wait to wear my new red dress. There was so much preparation. Emily and I had appointments for facials, manicures and pedicures. We were going to do our own makeup. I thought about a spray tan but decided against it because sometimes it looks fake. I even bought new shoes. Gotta go all out!

The nerves were getting to me as the week wore on. I knew SUPERSTAR wasn't the problem. It was all those people looking at me! I have to get this under control. I think it's a 90 second spot. I can do this. Chance tells me every five minutes, "You can do this."

Finally the day arrived. I have to say Emily and I looked fabulous. The photographers were lined up as we had our cars parked and walked in. I was praying no one wanted to talk to me before the show. I happened to walk in at about the same time as Miranda Lambert so all eyes were on her. Whew.

We got ourselves seated and I had a chance to freshen up. They told me my spot was half an hour into the show. I was starstruck looking at all the stars and Justin's face! I told him next year he'd be on the show for sure.

The lights dimmed and the two hosts were announced. Carrie Underwood and Reba McEntire appeared from behind the curtains. There was thunderous applause. Their opening words were informative and funny at the same time. They welcomed everyone and introduced the presenter for "Single of the Year." After that the first performer was Blake Shelton. Now I was really nervous and I squeezed Chance's hand.

There was a commercial and I knew I was next. Chance kept saying "Breathe, breathe..." but before we knew it, I heard my name called to go up on stage. I prayed I wouldn't trip. The lights were aimed at me and the first bars of SUPERSTAR were played. I relaxed all of a sudden and enjoyed the fleeting moment.

The turning stage made one full circle. Chance grabbed my hand so I didn't fall on the steps. It was over so fast.

There were hugs all around and then we just relaxed and enjoyed the rest of the show. Cassidy was so excited she wanted to practically sit on top of me. It was a wonderful fun experience. Marty said people were impressed. I was surprised. Wow, really?

After the show, we went into one of the restaurants and had a drink. Everyone toasted me and I was very happy.

Chance said, "This is just the beginning Becky, you're going to be a big star."

I kissed him and said, "Let's go home."

I noticed how Emily and Justin were looking at each other and I smiled because my friend was so happy.

Chapter 52

Our little Cassidy was starting school soon. There was an elementary school a couple blocks away from the ranch, which had all-day kindergarten three days a week. Chance took her to see the school and enrolled her in the class. We made a big deal out of her being so grown up and all. There would be twelve children in her class, seven girls and five boys. I knew when the first day came that Chance and I would cry our eyes out, but we kept a stiff upper lip around her so she wouldn't know.

I took her school shopping and bought her a new backpack. She wanted a pink one and I found a really pretty one. I got her some new clothes and a new pair of cowboy boots. I was in love with this child. Chance noticed and said it made him very happy to see how close we were.

Meanwhile Carrie continued her rehab up north but didn't seem to be improving. Cassidy didn't ask about her mother much any more.

Before we knew it, it was time for my next doctor appointment. Emily had a notebook full of information. The doctor was impressed so much of my memory had returned and said the remaining memories should all come back, even though it might take some time. He didn't need to see me again.

Emily would bring up something we had done together over the years and have me talk about it. My memory about the Silver Eagle trips was a bit sketchy but I remembered enough to be mortified at the way I chased Johnny all over the place. I needed to give myself a break and stop beating myself up about it.

Justin and Emily were becoming somewhat serious. They were spending a lot of time together when she wasn't working at the dude ranch. More often than not, her nights were spent at the trailer with him, giving Chance and me some much needed privacy. Cassidy stayed overnight when she didn't have school the next day. She loved going to school and had play dates set up with her classmates all the time. Justin was working on his first CD and my album was due to be released in two months. Chance and I were solid. Things were just humming along.

Chance was getting ready for the big two-day rodeo in Gatlinburg. He kept asking me to go with him but I had promised Emily we'd spend some girl time together. In retrospect I should have gone with him.

Meanwhile, Justin had secretly called his father and told him Chance would be leaving for the rodeo in a few days. Johnny made plane reservations immediately and arrived in Nashville the next day.

Chapter 53

Justin didn't tell Emily his father was coming because he knew she'd tell me. Chance was ready to leave for Gatlinburg and I was having a hard time with it. We had never been apart. I kept touching him, wanting him to stay. I knew he couldn't but I tried to make him understand how much I would miss him. He kissed me goodbye and gave me a big bear hug.

"I'll be back in three days. You and Emily go and have some fun." I smiled through my tears and told him to have a good time. I felt the tears on my cheek as I watched him go up the driveway.

Emily came home and could see how upset I was. She said it would be like the old days, when it was just her and me. No Chance, no Justin. This made me smile. We made appointments for a spa day.

When we returned from our relaxing day, I noticed Justin and Marty talking with someone over by the bunkhouse.

"Who's that?" I asked Emily.

She said it was probably a guest from the dude ranch. We went into the house to change our clothes and get ready for a horseback ride. It was a wonderful way to end the day. I missed Chance but I knew he was working hard doing something he loved. We walked up the dirt road toward the stables and Justin waved as we approached. Marty had gone back in the house but the stranger was still with Justin. He walked over to us and gave Emily a hug as my eyes were fixed on the other man. A smile came over the man's face as he saw me and I realized it was Justin's father, Johnny. I grabbed Emily's arm and choked out, "What's he doing here!"

Johnny said hello to us like it was no big deal. I looked at him and remembered how handsome he was and how his smile took my breath away.

Emily lashed out at Justin, "Why didn't you tell us he was coming?"

I turned and started to walk away but Johnny called out to me not to leave, he just wanted to talk. I felt sick as I realized they had planned the whole thing for when Chance was away.

"I have nothing to say to you," I said, as Emily and I walked to my car and drove away. She was furious with Justin and I felt pretty much the same way. "Maybe Johnny will leave now," I said.

Unbeknownst to us, the conversation between Johnny and Marty centered around Marty offering Johnny a job at the ranch. They really hit it off and Marty asked him if he could move in with Justin and be an all around handyman. There was always something needing to be fixed. Justin wasn't crazy about the idea because of privacy issues with Emily, but what could he say?

Emily and I did some shopping and came home. I thought for sure Johnny would be gone by the time we got back. Justin met us as we drove in and told us his father had gone to the airport to fly to

Atlanta but he would be back the next day to start his new job. I don't know who was more shocked, me or Emily. I couldn't imagine Johnny being around all the time and went into the main house to tell Marty it wasn't a good idea. Marty insisted on a trial run for a month to see how it worked out. He needed help and told me to just deal with it. Usually Marty is more understanding than this and I was very disappointed.

"Wait 'til Chance gets back and finds out about this," I said to Emily.

She was more concerned about her love life with Justin, which will now be non-existent. I told her she'd have to be with him at our house in her bedroom. There was no other choice. Emily was hopping mad at Justin and I could hear her all the way from the barn. It wasn't his fault but she was mad about him not telling her his father was coming. This blindsided me and it wasn't fair. How did such a good day do a complete 180?

Little did I know but Johnny was completely blown away when he saw me. He thought I looked better than ever. It was difficult for him to see me with another man. He watched from afar and could tell I seemed happy with the big cowboy. He still didn't believe it. He was a stubborn man.

Justin really wanted his father to leave so he could be with Emily. Finally Johnny left after asking Justin if he could figure out a day when Chance wasn't around so he could fly up and see him and at the same time see me. Justin said he'd try but Chance was around pretty much all the time. He remembered, though, that there was a rodeo coming up in Gatlinburg in a few weeks so maybe that would be a good time. Chance would be gone for the weekend and he didn't think I was going with him. After all, Emily and I wanted some girl time away from the boys. The father and son hugged each other when they said goodbye and Justin said he would let him know.

Johnny still felt I cared about him and he just wanted to talk to me. What would it hurt? If I told him I was happy, he would have to leave me alone.

Meanwhile Marty wanted Justin to record his music and get it out there. I knew when Marty wanted something to be done that he wouldn't quit. Justin agreed to pick three songs and learn the arrangements. He was very excited and couldn't wait to get started. He didn't seem to care how much work was involved. He was ready.

Justin was moving things around and making room for his father in the trailer. It wasn't going to be comfortable for sure. Emily asked Marty if Johnny could have a room in the main house. He certainly wasn't going to stay in the bunkhouse and the trailer was just too small. She had a point but Marty knew why she was asking. It had everything to do with her and Justin. He said he'd talk to Dixie about this and they would decide by the time Johnny got back the next day.

Emily and I hung out in the dude ranch dining room and got something to eat. We didn't do this very often but I needed to talk to her.

"I can't imagine seeing Johnny every day and acting like he was just another hired hand." Emily responded, "Just stay away from him. The ranch is big enough, you don't have to ever see him."

By the time Johnny got back the next day, Marty had decided he could have a room in the main house on the first floor by the laundry. There was a bathroom there so it would be comfortable for him. All of the help had meals included in their pay. Justin told his father about this when he arrived at the ranch. I made myself scarce by working with the horses in the back pasture. Emily drove back and told me he had arrived. I just shook my head and prayed for the next day to come so Chance would be home.

Chapter 54

Chance arrived the next afternoon and when he saw me he picked me up and spun me around. I had tears on my face. I was so happy. Out of the corner of my eye I could see Johnny watching us as he fixed some fence over by the main house. Chance didn't see him at first but as he parked his truck, he almost ran into him. He asked Johnny what he was doing and almost flipped out when he told him he had just started working there. Justin was there in a flash and intervened so there wasn't any trouble. Chance and I walked up to my house, shut the door and pulled the drapes shut. Chance wanted to know how this happened.

"I go away for a couple days and this guy shows up. What was Marty thinking?"

I told him Emily had asked Marty if Johnny could stay in the main house instead of in the trailer with Justin. Chance laughed and said he could certainly understand why she didn't want him sharing the small trailer.

I was so happy Chance was back. He had a great rodeo with a big crowd and a lot of press. There were no accidents and everything went smoothly. He said he missed me and made me promise I'd go with him the next time. He realized that Justin had told his father that he would be away for a couple days. I told him it didn't matter. I didn't want anything to do with him. We made love but I couldn't relax because Johnny was so close. Chance said he would have to do something about this and soon. What could he do? He said he'd have a talk with Johnny when he returned and make sure he knew I was going to be his wife.

"I don't care if you two are friends if it's possible," he said, "as long as you aren't friends with benefits." I assured him there was no problem on my end.

Later that night I had a vivid dream of my momma sitting out by the horses on an old bench. I could see her so clearly and tears fell as we hugged each other. She said she wanted to be sure I appreciated what a good man Chance was and she wanted me to have a life with him. She knew he would take care of me and any children we might have. All of a sudden she faded from view and was gone. I woke up and saw Chance sleeping beside me and thanked my momma for her wise words. I could feel goosebumps everywhere. Chance stirred and asked if everything was all right. I whispered to him that everything was just perfect.

We had a lot of guests scheduled for the next week and Emily and I would be very busy. The next afternoon I noticed Johnny was back and Chance had walked up to Justin's trailer. They didn't talk very long and shook hands so I assumed there wasn't going to be any bloodshed. When I asked Chance what he said, he just said it was guy talk.

Emily and I walked up to the main house to see Dixie and we ran right into Johnny coming out of his room. We were all very pleasant to each other but I sensed he wanted to talk to me alone. Johnny told Justin he was going to hang out at The

Hummingbird that night. He had talked to Marty about tending bar a couple nights a week for extra money. I thought, "Boy, the tourists are going to love him."

Emily steered me away and said, "Let's get the boys and go get something to eat."

We piled into Chance's truck and went down to the diner. Chance told us all about the rodeo and Justin listened wide-eyed. He had no idea what a trick rider did.

Chapter 55

The envelope on the dining room table looked very official. Marty said it was delivered to the main house the day before and he had forgotten to mention it. I picked it up, put it in my bag and told Emily I would look at it later. We were going shopping in Nashville. There were sales all over the place! I needed some new makeup and skin cream with SPF 30. The summer sun was a killer. I had not seen Johnny since the night we ran into each other in the house. Marty told me he was busy fixing fences out in the back pastures. He thought it was probably a good idea to keep him busy away from the house until everyone got used to him being around.

    We were all going to The Hummingbird on Friday night. Justin was going to sing one of his new songs and Emily and I couldn't wait to hear him. Johnny was working behind the bar and I thanked Marty for the warning. I was going to sing SUPERSTAR. Any way you look at it, it would be weird. Emily would have her phone ready for pictures.

    Emily told me she was glad to have this time alone with me because she needed to talk to me. Justin had not talked much about his mother, Sharon, who lived in Atlanta. He told Emily that his mom had remarried a wealthy contractor, Roger

McCall, and they had a lovely home. He had mentioned Emily to her once or twice but realized his mother didn't approve because of the age difference.

"So this is Johnny's ex-wife, right?" I asked her.

Emily answered, "Yes, but you don't know the half of it. They're coming to Nashville when Justin's CD is released and they're going to stay at the dude ranch."

The words went over my head at first and then I understood what Emily had said.

"Do they even like horses? Why do they have to stay here? Tell Justin to find them someplace else to stay." Emily had already told him this but his mother insisted they would be staying here. I couldn't help but wonder what she looked like.

Emily was distraught and I could understand why. I told her, "We'll figure out what to do when we find out when they're coming. Maybe we won't have any rooms available or something." I wondered what Johnny thought about this. Life is complicated, no doubt about it. I felt like my past was being shoved in my face.

Marty had left me a message saying that it was looking more and more like Justin's CD and my album would be released near or on the same date. What a party this would be!

I had forgotten all about the envelope I had put in my bag earlier. The return address was from a law office in Coral Gables, Florida. Emily and I had stopped for coffee on the way home.

"What the heck is this, Emily? I've never been there in my life."

"Well, open it and find out!" Emily said impatiently.

I tore open the end of the envelope and opened the letter:

"*Dear Miss Steele, We regret to inform you that your ex-husband, Daniel Jackson, was killed in a motorcycle accident. We represent the estate in this matter. Mr. Jackson named you as the sole beneficiary in his will. We will need to verify your account number so we can deposit the check for $500,000.00. Please contact us at your earliest convenience. Yours truly, Behman, Copeland and Myers LLP*"

The blood drained out of my face and the room started to spin.

Emily put her hand on my arm. "What's wrong, oh my God, what's wrong!"

I handed her the letter and in about 15 seconds, she screamed. Everyone looked at us and the waitress came running over to see what had happened. I couldn't talk so Emily just said we had gotten a huge surprise.

Chapter 56

I was hyperventilating and couldn't catch my breath. As soon as I could, I reached for my phone and called Chance.

When he answered, I just said, "We're at the diner. Please come and get me now,"

Emily kept telling me to breathe and in a few minutes I calmed down. Chance tore into the parking lot and jumped out of his truck. I must have looked like I had seen a ghost or something. Emily said she would follow us back to the ranch. I still couldn't talk and make sense so I handed Chance the letter.

He yelled an expletive and grabbed me. "Becky, Becky OH MY GOD, BECKY !!!!!"

He called Marty and Dixie and told them to meet us at the main house. He just caught them as they were heading to The Hummingbird. Marty wondered if something had happened to one of us girls. Chance assured him everyone was okay.

My voice had come back.

"I'll believe it when I see the check. This must be a prank or something. He never had two nickels to rub together. Where would he get that kind of money?"

Chance said it didn't look like a joke and that I could call the law office from the ranch in a few minutes. It was the longest 30-minute ride in history. We all went into the house where Marty and Dixie were waiting for God knows what. I handed the letter to Marty.

Dixie made coffee and told us all to sit at the table. Out of the corner of my eye, I noticed Johnny wasn't around. Marty let out a huge roar as he read the letter.

"Well, I'll be damned. Call the law office and make sure it's for real."

I took a huge sip of coffee and grabbed Chance's hand. I asked him to dial the number for me. When someone answered the phone, I told them who I was and that I wanted to verify the facts in this letter. Within seconds, a man answered and said he was Frank Myers, one of the partners. He confirmed the letter was real and wanted to verify my bank information. He congratulated me and said he was sorry about my husband. I told him I would have my attorney contact him the next day.

I disconnected and looked at everyone staring at me. I didn't know whether to laugh or cry. I was in shock. Marty said he would call his lawyer first thing in the morning for me. He would take care of everything. I just wanted to go home and sit quietly and think. Any decisions could wait until tomorrow. Chance and Emily walked up the road to the house with me after I said goodbye to Marty and Dixie. I wondered how our lives would change now. Money has a way of screwing things up.

Emily grabbed her overnight bag and went to stay with Justin. I was glad to have the privacy with Chance. I kept trying to make some sense out of this windfall. What on earth am I going to do with all this money? Chance told me he was sure Marty had an investment broker to help. I knew he wanted to expand The Hummingbird and have an outdoor arena. Maybe I could help. Just having a plan made me feel better. I planned to talk to him in the morning. Chance and I cuddled on the couch and I fell fast asleep dreaming of dollar bills. I woke up in the middle of the night and we both went to bed. Any thoughts of Johnny were long gone. There was no doubt this was where I wanted to be.

Marty came outside the next morning when he saw us up by the dude ranch. He had talked to his lawyer who called the attorney in Coral Gables. They both agreed it would be better if I went in person with my ID to pick up the check. I turned to Chance and asked him to have his dad get us passes so we could fly there today. He called him immediately and his dad said we could be on a flight at noon. Marty said his attorney would call the law office in Coral Gables and tell them to expect us. Emily said she'd hold down the fort while I was gone. Luckily we didn't have a full house at the dude ranch.

There was not much time so I quickly took my dogs for a walk and changed my clothes. Marty had also made us a reservation for a rental car at the Miami Airport. Chance drove over to get me and off we went. We flew to Miami and picked up the car. It was only a 15-minute drive to Coral Gables.

I had never been there. What a lovely area. Palm trees were everywhere lining the streets and beautiful flowers were planted along all the sidewalks. We were ushered in like royalty at the law office. I barely had time to take my jacket off when Mr. Myers asked me for two forms of ID and had me sign something saying I received the money. He handed me the cashier's check and an envelope addressed "*To Becky.*"

We were out of there in ten minutes and on our way back to Miami to catch our flight back to Nashville. Marty was going to open an account at his bank for me where I could deposit the money. My head was whirling. Chance wanted me to open the envelope as soon as we turned in the rental car. There was a handwritten note inside. I had never noticed Danny had such nice handwriting.

"Dear Becky,
If you are reading this it means I've left this earth and am on my next journey. I never forgave myself all those years ago for deserting you and I hope this money will make up for some of the pain I caused you. I've never forgotten you and what a great woman you are. I really loved you and I hope you found happiness with someone else. This money came from my dad who made a lot of money in real estate. He left some of it to me so I'm leaving some of it to you. I hope you are happy and that you can forgive me. Maybe someday, who knows, our paths will cross again.
Love, Danny"

My eyes filled with tears as I put the note away. For a brief moment I was quiet and said a prayer for Danny. I had so many questions that now would never be answered.

I let Chance read the note and he said you could tell Danny had a good heart. He never asked any questions and told me if I wanted to talk about that time so long ago, he would be glad to listen. He hugged me and said there was a lot to think about.

"Think of all the good things you can do with this money."

I thought of my mother and how happy she would be about this inheritance. She never liked Danny and was upset when I married him. I wondered what she would think if she knew about this. She was always so worried about making ends meet and I'm sure she'd be glad I wouldn't have to worry about that ever again.

In no time we were back in Nashville and on the way to the ranch. Marty met us when we drove up the driveway. There was another car parked there which belonged to a friend of his who was an investment broker. There were decisions to be made but for now the money was going into my bank account. Emily saw us and walked over to tell me everything was going smoothly. She didn't ask any questions.

Chance had to leave to take Cassidy into school for something. Her kindergarten adventure had started on Monday.

I felt lost and unable to think straight. It would take a while to adjust to this. Marty and Dixie sat with me in the house and we had coffee. Thank God for these two wonderful souls who were looking out for me.

Chapter 57

Everything was a blur for a few days. I managed to keep up with chores and work around the ranch. Monday morning came quickly and I went with Chance when he dropped Cassidy off at school. She acted very grown up about this and looked so cute with her new backpack and sneakers. She waved goodbye to us and said she'd see us later. Chance had tears in his eyes. His baby was growing up so fast.

Emily wanted to have lunch so we could talk. We went down to the diner and ordered pizza. I was starving because I didn't eat the day before.

"What's the first thing you're going to buy?" she asked. I hadn't really thought much about it, but I really needed a new car. I would have Chance go with me to be sure the car salesman wasn't ripping me off. Is this the way it will be from now on, I thought. Once people find out you have money, everyone will have their hand out.

"Please don't tell anyone, at least for now." I told Emily. I had to get my priorities straight.

Marty was in the house when we got back and I asked him if he had time to talk.

"I've always got time for you, Becky."

I wanted to know if he had looked into buying the property for sale next to The Hummingbird. I was thinking we could build an outdoor arena for concerts big enough to seat at least 500 to a thousand people. Marty's eyes lit up.

"That's a great idea. There would have to be enough room for parking and the zoning would have to be changed. I'll get right on it," he replied. The idea of having big name artists performing there appealed to both of us. It was a dream right now, but an attainable dream for sure.

The record producer from Dream Big Nashville had left me a voicemail. My album was going to drop in two weeks at about the same time Justin's CD would be released. This was just what we wanted, both together. Mr. Barkley was busy doing the publicity. They would throw a big party at The Hummingbird. I called Justin and told him to get ready. It was happening! He thanked me for letting him know and mentioned that his mother and stepfather were definitely coming. I told him I would have to check to see if there was any available room at the dude ranch. I really hoped there wasn't.

When I told Emily about all this, she seemed calmer than she was when she first found out. She made appointments to have her hair cut and highlighted and bought some new clothes. She wanted to make a good first impression on Justin's folks.

Of course there was room for them at the dude ranch and there was nothing I could do to stop them from staying there. Justin seemed more nervous about it than Emily. Had anyone even told Johnny they were coming? Where had he been? I hadn't seen him in a while. I think Marty was just keeping him busy.

Chance and I picked up Cassidy after school. She was so excited and told us everything she did all day. I thought it would be difficult for her to be away from us for the day, but it didn't bother her one bit. She would be ready to go to bed early. Chance took her to his mom's for dinner and she decided she wanted to just stay there for the night. Five years old going on twenty.

Chapter 58

It was Friday night after a wild week and Justin and I were at The Hummingbird ready for the show. The place was packed. It was amazing! Justin already had a following and his CD wasn't even released yet. I noticed that he was very much his father's son and had inherited his good looks and great smile. No wonder Emily was smitten with him. We went up on stage together and I stepped to the side so he could sing one of his new songs. The applause was deafening.

I walked over to the microphone and motioned to Kenny. The boys started the introduction to SUPERSTAR. It seemed like every time we did this song it got better. The goosebumps were all over my body and I could see Johnny's face in my mind. There was no doubt now that I remembered him. It was unnerving to glance over at the bar and see him standing there, almost like a dream. But this was no dream! Johnny Munroe was so close that I could touch him. I avoided looking at him. The crowd erupted with applause and whistles. Justin and I took a bow and hugged each other. I could feel Johnny staring at me. Emily was smiling from ear to ear. It was a great night.

Chance was waiting when I got home. He wasn't able to go to the show because he had a parent teacher conference at Cassidy's school. He knew I would understand and of course I did. I told him I missed him standing at the bottom of the stairs waiting for me. He gave me a big hug. I really loved this man.

Emily made a pot of coffee. She wondered if I had heard that Johnny had a girlfriend, someone he met when he was tending bar at The Hummingbird. I didn't know but I wasn't surprised. I didn't think he could go very long without a woman in his life. Of course I wanted to know what she looked like. Emily said she'd ask Justin if he'd seen her. He was still at The Hummingbird enjoying all the attention. Chance just shook his head. I knew he wanted to tell me to mind my own business.

Later Emily and I were catching up while taking the dogs for a walk. It had become clear to me that my priorities had shifted.

"Emily," I started, "I don't think I will try out for Miss Rodeo Tennessee again. I just don't have time to compete with everything that's going on around here. I only rode in two rodeos this season."

Emily answered, "I understand, and it's totally up to you. You've got so much going on now! You didn't know about Chance or Cassidy when you applied, let alone everything else. It's okay. Don't feel guilty about it. This will give someone else a chance." I was glad she understood and it made me feel better.

Chapter 59

Marty called me up to the house to talk about the outdoor arena. He had a different idea. There was a big park across the street from The Hummingbird.

"How about we have a Hummingbird Concert Series in the Park instead?"

I thought it was a great idea! We could schedule them out and average one a month. Marty said we could expand the park because there were no buildings there. Parking would be on the next street over. It could hold up to 1000 spectators. He said this way all we'd have to do is build a stage and put in lighting and a parking area. People could bring their own chairs or sit on blankets. He said we would need a lawyer to put all of it in writing. This sounded exactly like what I imagined. Live Nation could handle the ticket sales online. I told him to tell me how much money he'd need to get started. He said he would get busy making phone calls. He knew someone that did this sort of thing and could pull it all together and supervise step by step. For now all we could do was put a sign up saying,

"COMING SOON
THE HUMMINGBIRD CONCERT
SERIES IN THE PARK"

I could hardly wait to tell Emily and Chance. I ran back to the house to tell Emily and ran right into

Chance who was leaving. I made him come back inside so I could tell them together. They loved the idea and were very excited. Chance said this would create jobs and put people to work. He was proud of me for doing this. I told him it was Marty's idea and I was just along for the ride.

Emily went up to see Justin and found him with his father out by the bunkhouse. They both agreed it was a great idea. Johnny wanted to know where I got the money to finance this and Emily told him about the inheritance.

Shaking his head he said, "That Becky. She's always one step ahead." He never even knew I had been married before.

By the time I got back up to the house, Marty had lined up an excavator and hired a project manager to oversee everything. We were wasting no time! His lawyer was on the way with a contract for us to sign so everything would be legal between us. I hadn't given a thought to the incoming revenue but I trusted Marty completely. However he wanted to split was okay with me. Dixie was busy on the computer creating a bookkeeping system. She knew how to record expenses and track income. She called her sister Doreen and offered her a job taking care of the books. I had met her before and was happy she would be on board. Things were moving right along. Almost too fast.

The project manager whose name was Mark told us that he would hire the contracting firm to build the stage and set up the lighting. Mark and Marty would put their heads together on the best way to do this. I had a vision of this in my head and it was quickly becoming real.

Chance, Justin and Emily joined me for lunch at The Trick Pony. We were on the verge of something huge but meanwhile we had our big release party coming up fast. There were a million questions and I didn't know how to answer all of them. Chance was going to ask Marty about hiring security. He would take care of all the details. My head was spinning from all the excitement and I couldn't wait to be alone with him that night for some peace and quiet. So many lives would be touched by these concerts and I said a silent thank you prayer to Danny for this wonderful gift.

Chapter 60

The release party was scheduled for the next weekend right after my album dropped. Justin's CD would be released the next day. The record company had signs made for the whole block and put up tons of balloons that said "Congrats Becky" and "Congrats Justin." The party was talked about on social media and was creating quite a stir. People were coming from out of town as the reservations poured in for the Gaylord Opryland Hotel and the other hotels in the area. I was a bit overwhelmed.

"Emily," I said to my best friend over coffee, "Wouldn't you think Justin's Mom and stepfather would rather stay at a big hotel instead of at the ranch?" Emily agreed but there was nothing she could do. We were going to have to deal with them whether we liked it or not. They were coming the next week and were already booked at the dude ranch. Emily was trying her best to stay calm. I wasn't thrilled about it either. I felt sorry for Justin who was stuck in the middle. Emily told me Johnny was indifferent to the whole situation and just wanted to steer clear of Justin's mother.

We decided to all go down to the park to see the start of the excavation and the groundbreaking for the stage. Marty had a big smile on his face and gave me a bear hug. Chance was busy interviewing security personnel. Emily and Justin stood with me and we just took it all in. It was really happening. A crowd had gathered and everyone seemed pretty excited. The sign was brought in on a truck and placed near the road ... "SITE FOR HUMMINGBIRD CONCERT SERIES, COMING SOON" Posted was a phone number to Dixie and Doreen if anyone had questions. I was very happy I didn't have to answer the phones.

Emily teased, "You're kidding right? You're funding this. No one would expect you to answer the phones!"

Old habits die hard.

Chapter 61

The days were flying by. The big launch party was right around the corner. Emily tripped over her own feet that morning, running to find me in the corral with Skipper. She wanted to tell me Justin's mom and stepfather had arrived.

"What does she look like?" I inquired.

Emily answered, "Come see for yourself. They're in the dining room having breakfast."

I told her I'd meet her there in a few minutes. I was glad I looked presentable enough so I didn't have to change my clothes.

I asked Ryan to unsaddle Skipper and turn him out to pasture. For some reason I thought of Cassidy and the fact that she wasn't around much now since she was in school. I really missed her.

As I was walking over to the dude ranch, I ran right into Johnny coming out of the house. There was no place to hide so I tried to be civil and asked if he knew Justin's mom had arrived. He said he was headed for the dining room to have breakfast with them. He asked me if I would join them. I tried not to make a face and said that I was meeting Emily who had just caught up with us. All of a sudden I wanted to go somewhere else, anywhere else. Emily asked me to go in the house with her as an excuse to get away from Johnny.

"Thanks for the save, Em," I told her, "but I still want to see what Justin's mom looks like."

She said to not be a chicken and just walk right in and go through into the kitchen. "We don't have to stay."

Marty wanted to know what we were up to. I laughed and just told him "girl stuff."

We waited about five minutes and then walked up onto the porch and through the sliding glass doors. The problem was everyone working knew us and made a point of saying hello. I kept a smile on my face as I glanced around the dining room. Johnny was watching us too. I tried not to stare but Sharon and Roger McCall were sure a striking couple. Sharon's blond short hair was streaked and you could tell she went to an expensive salon. You could also tell they had money. Her husband was very handsome with salt and pepper hair. Emily and I made an excuse to grab some doughnuts and walked back to the kitchen. Sharon McCall was standing next to Johnny as we walked by.

I whispered to Emily, "Do you think she has a spray tan?" I noticed she was in really good shape and you could tell she took excellent care of herself. I was surprised, to tell the truth, that Johnny wasn't still with her. I know it's not all about looks. We got the hell out of there and started to walk back to the house.

Emily wanted to know what I thought.

"She is very attractive and I expected nothing less. Justin told me his mother spent a fortune on clothes and makeup. It shows."

Chance was getting out of his truck as we left the dude ranch. He asked what we were doing and why I had a strange look on my face.

I kissed him and said, "I'll tell you later. Do you think you could bring Cassidy over after school for a pony ride?"

He said "Sure, we will see you later."

Cassidy was so excited to see Lollipop and me. I wasn't sure which one of us was her favorite. I grabbed her and gave her a big hug as I lifted her up into the saddle. She told me how much she loved her school and all the fun things they did. Chance caught up with us and walked her around the corral a few times. I watched and could feel the love in my heart for both of them. Then the three of us went down to the diner for breakfast. I don't think Cassidy ever stopped talking. She was so happy when we were all together. I kept forgetting with everything going on to ask Chance if he had heard anything about her mother. Things were crazy enough without her getting out of rehab and coming down here.

Chapter 62

It was the night of the big launch party! My clothes were all laid out and I had decided to do my own makeup. Emily always said I did a better job than the pros anyway. Justin came over and wanted me to help him calm down but I told him to get used to the nerves because they were part of the whole experience. I told him he was going to be great. I made Emily promise to stay close in case anything unforeseen happened. There were a lot of players in the pot tonight.

We got to The Hummingbird early and I was shocked at how many people were already there. The crowd had spilled out into the parking lot. Marty had known this would happen so he put speakers on the outside of the building so people could hear. Justin was sitting with his mother and stepfather and Johnny was behind the bar with Kelsey working. Chance was all over the place and had two extra men in attendance in case anyone got drunk and started a fight or something.

Marty turned down the lights and welcomed everyone. He introduced Justin to a huge round of applause and then he called me up on stage. It was quite a moment and I almost lost it. Everyone started chanting, "Becky! Becky! Becky!" It was crazy.

Kenny started the intro to Justin's song and the crowd calmed down. I stood in the background and watched. I could see how proud his mother was and Johnny was beaming all over. He sang his heart out as if he had been doing this for years. He was already a star and I was sure he was going to go as far as he wanted to in this business. Marty shook his hand as the crowd went nuts. Mr. Barkley knew he had a winner for his label.

Marty started to introduce me but as soon as I moved the crowd started whistling and clapping. I took my guitar from Emily and put it over my shoulder as Kenny and the boys started the haunting intro to SUPERSTAR. I noticed Johnny staring at me and I tried to ignore him as I started to sing. Chance was on one side of the stairs and Justin was on the other. Something came over me as I poured my heart into this heartbreaking song. I glanced over at Johnny and for a moment made eye contact as the goosebumps and whispers took over. It was like we were back in the Silver Eagle days. I was frozen in time for a minute until I realized that both Chance and Sharon had seen the connection between Johnny and me.

All of a sudden there was some commotion. Sharon was sitting at a nearby table and staggered to the stage, drunk. Chance grabbed her but not before she tripped and threw her drink at me. She was off balance and the vodka cranberry hit Justin right in the face. Chance just barely stopped her from falling headfirst.

Justin screamed at his mother, "What the hell are you doing?"

The whole debacle took about 15 seconds. I was frozen in place. The energy of the crowd that had gotten quiet while I was singing changed to craziness in an instant. Marty grabbed the mic and asked everyone to please be seated. Johnny went over to Sharon and with her husband's help got her away from the stage. Emily came to me and asked if I was all right. I looked at her and we both burst out laughing. Sharon showed her true colors. I loved it. Justin told her to get out and go back to Atlanta that very night. With all the media attention, he was going to come out of this smelling like a rose. There is no such thing as bad publicity.

Marty thanked everyone for coming and opened up the bar for drinks on the house. I went backstage with Justin and the band until everything calmed down. Emily came back and told us that Sharon and her husband had left. Chance was at the door making sure she didn't turn around and come back.

It was not a rowdy crowd, thank goodness, and there was a steady stream of music from my new album entertaining everyone. I grabbed Emily and asked her if she thought Chance was mad at me for what happened. I didn't mean anything. I just got caught up in the moment. She told me not to waste my breath talking to her, I just better talk to Chance. Johnny and Kelsey were busy pouring drinks. I didn't have a good feeling about this and wanted to go home with Chance. I asked Emily to get him. Justin was having a blast and wanted to stay which was fine with me. I had had enough excitement for one night.

Chance came backstage and said he could leave whenever I did. The other two security guys could handle everything from here. I told Emily we were leaving and that I would see her in the morning. Johnny glanced at me but I looked away. I quickly gave Marty a hug as we ducked out the side door. I certainly never expected anything like this to happen.

The first thing I asked Chance when we got into the truck was if he was mad over what happened. He put his arm around me and said no he understood how music can get to you sometimes. Whew. I was worried. He said the emotion is what drives SUPERSTAR and makes it such a great hit. We laughed at Sharon's reaction and what an ass she made out of herself. I snuggled up to him and told him I loved him.

He responded quickly, "I love you too, you know that. Stop worrying. I won't let a little thing like this come between us."

How did I get so lucky to have a man like Chance?

We were happy that Emily was staying with Justin so we had our privacy. What a crazy night it was.

Chapter 63

The next morning Emily came over and said Sharon's trip on the stairs of the stage was all over social media. She must've been so embarrassed. Emily said they cleared out of the dude ranch in the middle of the night.

"Did they pay their bill?" I couldn't help but ask.

Emily replied, "Yes, and they even left tips for the staff."

Big of her, I thought. "Just think, Emily, I saved you from having to deal with Justin's mother."

She laughed and told me she owed me.

I hoped Marty wasn't having a fit. He wasn't. He sent me a text saying The Hummingbird was all over the news. "Attaway Becky!"

Chance was taking Cassidy to school and had to run some errands so he was already gone. That gave Emily and me time to talk.

The first thing she asked was, "Do you have old feelings for Johnny? When I answered, "no" a hundred times, she asked, "Then why did you do that?" I was trying to be patient.

"Emily, it was just a moment in time that didn't mean anything." She didn't believe me and said she saw it plain as day. She couldn't believe Chance wasn't mad about it. My patience was gone so I answered a little too loud, "Well, he's not, so let's just forget it."

Emily retorted, "Johnny is not going to forget it, you can bet on that."

I didn't see Johnny anywhere. I hoped he had a day off and wouldn't be around. I asked Emily how Justin was. She said that other than being embarrassed about his mother, he was happy and excited at how well he was received. I'm telling you this kid was the real deal.

I really wanted to go see how the construction was coming along but thought we'd better wait a while until this incident at The Hummingbird was forgotten.

It was such a beautiful day. I took my dogs for a walk up to a far pasture. They were so happy and kept running to me and taking off. I loved these dogs so much. I didn't hear anyone behind me until one of the dogs barked to alert me. I turned around to see Johnny right behind me.

"What are you doing here?" I asked.

He said he just wanted to talk and he hadn't been able to get me alone since he moved in. He didn't look like he was going to do anything stupid so I said okay, but just for a few minutes. He asked me if last night was any kind of a sign that I still cared about him. I said, "No, it was just a memory from days gone by and the music brought it back. That's all it was." I told him I loved Chance and was going to marry him.

He said, "You thought you loved Mike too, and that didn't last."

I told him Mike was a rebound from him. I could tell by the look on his face I hit a nerve. I continued, glad to be able to say this after all this time.

"Chance is different. I'm different now too and we can have a good life together if you leave us alone. Please Johnny, let us be. Leave the past in the past. I was young and vulnerable and you took advantage of that. The feelings just aren't there anymore. I'm not sure it was ever real and maybe it was all just a fantasy."

He turned to walk away but instead came over to me and kissed me. I felt something stir inside of me but I pushed him away. I was close to tears.

"Please, Johnny, please leave me alone. Just remember the good times we had. A piece of me will always love you. But please, let it go."

He shook his head and walked back toward the house. He turned to look at me one last time. I stood there while my eyes filled with tears for the relationship that could have been. It was too late now. My heart belonged to Chance.

Meanwhile Chance had returned from his errands and was looking for me. He knew I was around because my car was parked by the house. He asked Emily where I was and she said I just wanted to clear my head so I went for a walk with my dogs. He saw Johnny coming up the road toward the ranch and wondered if I had been with him. A couple minutes later he saw my shelties running toward him and he knew I was on the way.

I saw him up ahead and waved. He walked toward me and we hugged each other. He asked about Johnny and I told him what I had said to him, that my life was with my fiancé. Chance smiled from ear to ear with relief, I think, and asked me if I wanted to go grab a fast bite at the diner.

I said, "Sure, after I change my clothes."

He came into the house with me and waited until I was ready. I put on a dark wig and a ball cap so no one would recognize me (I hoped). We could check out the construction from the road. Emily waved as we went up the driveway.

At the diner we sat in a booth away from the front door behind an older couple. Chance poked me as he realized the couple was talking about what happened at The Hummingbird the night before. I smiled as I listened to their version, which wasn't exactly true but interesting nevertheless. They couldn't figure out who Sharon was throwing the drink at. I guess if you didn't know the players it would be hard to piece it together.

We had a quick bite and then went over to see the construction. You could already see where the stage was going to be. The trusses were up for the roof and the lighting was in the works. The big sign was in place and could easily be seen from the road. There was a big mound of dirt where the grass was going to be extended to make room for seating.

Marty walked over from The Hummingbird when he saw us. The launch party had been a great success. The bar, even with the free drinks brought in a huge amount of money. He laughed and said there should be an uproar like what happened every night. He said everything was on schedule for the concert series and he was thinking about who he wanted to schedule on opening night. He wanted my two cents. Sugarland came to my mind immediately.

"I've got other news to tell you that I think will make everyone happy," he continued. He had decided to move Johnny to a room upstairs from The Hummingbird so he could be involved not only as a bartender but also in the day to day workings of the concert series.

"I think it will be the best thing for everyone and Johnny will be a big help if he is close by."

I had all I could do not to jump up and down, I was so relieved and happy. Chance was even happier than I was. Justin could see his father down here whenever he wanted to and I could relax and not worry about running into him all the time. I wondered if Emily knew. Things really do have a way of working out for the best.

Chapter 64

Meanwhile back at the ranch, Johnny had packed up his clothes and a few belongings and put them into the trunk of his car. He was not happy that Marty had asked him to move into Nashville and live upstairs over The Hummingbird. He considered quitting and going back home to Georgia but the thought of never seeing Becky again made him crazy. What did she see in that cowboy anyway? He remembered all their nights together and couldn't believe that she didn't want him anymore. He couldn't think of her with another man without getting really angry. He didn't understand his son with Emily either. After all, she was old enough to be his mother! Justin was too smart to be roped into a cougar affair. She was just after his money. She knows he'll be a big recording artist before long.

There was no one around when he was all packed up and ready to leave. He walked back to his room to be sure he hadn't forgotten anything. As he walked out to his car his eye caught something off to the side of the stairs. It looked like a small case of some kind. When he bent over to pick it up, he saw it was a billfold filled with money. He looked around to see if anyone from the dude ranch had dropped it. There were people around the other side that he could hear but no one he could see. He had never stolen anything in his life but something came over him and he quickly took the cash and threw the billfold into the driveway. He then got into his car and sped away.

Ryan was outside by the bunkhouse and noticed him leaving. He wondered why he was in such a hurry. When Johnny pulled over and looked at the bills a few miles down the road, he counted $600 in 100's and 50's. In his mind he thought, "If it's Marty's, it serves him right for kicking me out. He'll never miss it. These people are loaded."

The billfold did turn out to be Marty's. When he realized he had dropped it, he retraced his steps and found it empty in the driveway. He was shocked that someone had stolen the money. This cash was for the security detail at the concert site.

The next morning, Marty asked around to see if anyone had found the money. He assumed most people were honest and this was really bothering him. He walked by Johnny's room and noticed he had packed up his things. He thought it strange that he hadn't seen him at The Hummingbird the night before.

He then walked down the road to talk to Chance who was just leaving my house. Chance waited when he saw Marty coming. When he told him about the stolen money, Chance was surprised and thought maybe a guest had taken it. Marty shook his head and said he didn't think so. He got Ryan's attention as he was driving by with the feed truck. He asked him if he saw anyone lurking around the night before. Ryan said no, but he did notice Johnny hightailing it up the driveway in an awful hurry. Marty made a mental note to check Johnny's room at The Hummingbird when he was tending bar the next day. He didn't want to say anything to anyone yet, not until he figured out who had done this.

Emily and Justin waved as they drove up the driveway on the way to breakfast. They asked me to go but I had gotten a message from Marty that he wanted to see me and I was on my way up to the main house. Marty asked me to sit down and to keep what he was going to say between us. I thought uh oh something's not right. He proceeded to tell me about the missing money. Something told him that Johnny had taken it. I was really surprised because I always thought Johnny was an honest man. Marty said he had to find out and he would fire him if it were true.

Marty went into The Hummingbird earlier than usual because he wanted to keep an eye on Johnny. When the bar filled up around five, he sent Kelsey on an errand so Johnny would not be able to leave the bar. He went up the back stairs and quietly unlocked the door to Johnny's room. He was surprised at how neat it was. Johnny had hung up his clothes and put his things in a dresser. Marty opened the drawers one by one. The drawer on the bottom was off the track and hard to open. There were cards and a watch and other personal items casually lying in there. Marty started to close the drawer and pulled it back onto the track. He then thought he better put it back the way he found it. When he reached underneath to move the drawer off the track, he felt the cash. He pulled out $500.00. He knew this wasn't money Johnny had saved from working downstairs because he always paid the help in twenties. He also knew it wasn't tip money. No one tips with 50's or 100's. He gingerly put the money back under the drawer and locked the door when he left. He went downstairs and left by the side door. He texted me while I was at the ranch and told me to stay there because he had to talk to me. He told me to find Chance and have him meet us. I sensed that he had found the money.

Chapter 65

Chance and Marty met me at the big house. Marty explained how he had found most of the money in Johnny's room. I asked if he was going to fire him. Marty said, "Not yet." He wanted to set a trap and see if Johnny fell for it. He was going to put a few hundred dollars in a money bag and leave it under the bar. When Johnny cleaned up the next night he would find it. Kelsey wasn't working so she would not be involved. Chance said he would be in the bar at night and watch him without being seen. I was upset that Johnny had gone to the dark side. I had never seen this side of him.

Marty placed the money in the bag and put it near the bar sink. Johnny was due on in about half an hour. Chance had some of his friends come down so it wouldn't look strange if he was there for most of the night. I decided to stay away. I didn't want any part of this. The Hummingbird was quiet as the evening wore on and Marty announced they were closing early to have the floors cleaned. Chance and his friends left but he came back around and in the side door. Johnny was washing glasses and ringing out the cash register. Two guys arrived with mops and pails and began mopping the floor. Chance stood over by the exit where he couldn't be seen.

It was a perfect trap. As Johnny put the glasses away he saw the bag. He didn't hesitate and put the bag into his jacket pocket. Chance saw him but didn't react. He quietly ducked out the door and texted Marty. "Got him."

Marty confronted Johnny the next morning. He told him to get his things and get the hell off of his property. He said he'd keep his wages to make up for the money he stole. He told him he was lucky he wasn't having him arrested. He also said he wasn't welcome anywhere close to him or his property. Johnny didn't protest. He just gathered his stuff and left. When I heard what happened I told Chance that there was more to this. Johnny wouldn't just quietly walk away. I told Emily what happened knowing that she would tell Justin.

Johnny found a room a few blocks away but with no job and no money he realized he would have to go back to Georgia. After Emily told Justin what happened, he went into the bars around The Hummingbird and found his father. He was mad as hell and told him to leave and not come back. Johnny made a nasty comment about Emily and Justin punched him. Then he grabbed him and pushed him out the door. Justin was stronger than he looked.

Marty needed a bartender and hired one of Kelsey's friends to pick up the slack. It was fun having two attractive women behind the bar and business picked up.

I told Chance that Johnny apparently had a temper and who knows what he would do. Chance said he'd keep an eye out but didn't think he was stupid enough to do something crazy. I said I hoped he was right.

We all went over the next morning to see how the construction was coming along. The stage was almost finished, the lights were in place and the landscaping was complete. What a beautiful park with flowers everywhere! I told Marty he better think about booking some performers sooner than later. Marty made some phone calls and booked Sugarland in two weeks for the first concert and three weeks later, he was able to secure Tim McGraw. The concert series was off and running. Marty said he would book three more shows three weeks apart. The shows were on Saturday nights at 8 p.m. Marty asked if Justin and I would do a number as an opening act. What a great opportunity! We happily agreed.

A week later the construction on the stage was completed. Marty increased the publicity and had pictures of Sugarland and Tim McGraw everywhere. I was so excited. Sugarland was my all time favorite. The next three performances for the concert series would be Dierks Bentley, Carly Pearce and Kelsea Ballerini! What a lineup! The ticket sales were through the roof. We were just praying it didn't rain.

Back in Nashville, Justin was as excited about the first concert as I was. We decided what songs we would sing to open the shows. This would be so much fun! We would do a short duet and then each of us would sing one song solo. Perfect.

Julie was out shopping for clothes for me. Sparkly and short. New white boots. New white hat. Spray tan. I was ready.

The week flew by. There were people everywhere checking out the park and the new stage. Chance had his security detail on high alert watching for any sign of trouble. Over 1,000 people were expected to see the first show. I kept asking him what kind of trouble. All he would say is that people are crazy and could do most anything. He assured me that everyone would be safe on his watch. Cassidy would be staying with his mom and dad and they would take good care of her.

Chance told me a couple days later that Carrie was still in rehab with no date for release. She wasn't doing well and seemed to have a death wish. The staff watched her 24/7. Cassidy had stopped asking for her mother. Chance decided to contact a lawyer and ask for full custody. There was nothing else he could do. After all, Cassidy was thriving and loved her new school and her new life. She was surrounded by people who loved her.

Chapter 66

The day arrived for the first concert. There were wall-to-wall people around the stage area. The police had set up traffic barricades to keep everything in order. Sugarland had arrived in the middle of the night. Their bus was parked over on the other side of the park. Marty had closed The Hummingbird at noon. He took me over to the stage to meet Jennifer and Kristian of Sugarland. I could hardly breathe and didn't want to make a fool of myself. They were both so kind and complimented ME on my music. Can you imagine?

The construction crew had built a wall behind the stage entrance so the public could not access the stage. There was a guard there at all times. A small dressing room was tucked away for emergencies. There were two steps up to the entryway to the stage.

Emily kept trying to get me to eat something but I was too excited. We had to go home and get dressed! Time was going fast! I told Chance I'd be back in a flash. He was so busy I don't think he even heard me.

It was people as far as the eye could see and it was still two hours till show time. People had brought blankets and folding chairs. There was a big sign saying, NO ALCOHOL ALLOWED. I wondered how many would sneak it in anyway.

Chance was all over the place. He was on his phone constantly. Around 7 pm he made a sweep of the front of the stage. Something caught his eye. There was a man in a hoodie walking away very fast from the rear wall of the stage. He thought to himself, "Who wears a hoodie? It's 85 degrees." The hair on the back of his neck stood up. He raced to the back wall past the guard onto the rear grass near the stage entrance. He would tell me later he had no idea what he was looking for but he knew something wasn't right.

Under the steps he saw it. A small duffel bag with a ticking noise. He screamed "JOKER 5!" into his phone, which brought two undercover bomb squad cops running. The time was set for 8 pm, just when Justin and I would be beginning our performances. Whoever this creep was, he didn't know much about making bombs because the bomb squad had it diffused in about five minutes. Chance put it in his truck along with the duffel bag for evidence.

Chance called his men out in the parking lots and told them to find this guy. One of them saw him drive away and was trying to chase him. Chance had a hunch and told them to head for the airport.

Now understand no one in the crowd had any idea this drama was playing out in the back of the stage. I thought it strange I hadn't seen Chance for a while but I was too busy myself to give it much thought. Sound checks were done and Justin and I came out onto the stage at exactly 8 pm. The crowd was going crazy. Our performances were spot on and we stayed out about a half hour longer to give autographs. After another sound check around 9 pm, the lights dimmed and Sugarland came running out from behind the curtain to the roar of the crowd. It was deafening. They threw guitar picks into the crowd of fans and had a ball. What a great 45-minute set. They performed old and new music and the crowd just loved every minute of their performance. I was delirious with joy!

Marty caught up with me and asked where Chance was. I had no idea. No one had seen him for a while. This was because Chance was at the Nashville airport with two of his men trying to get a plane that was out on the taxiway to return to the gate. He flashed his ID and the operations personnel told the pilot to turn around. Official Police business. The hooded stranger had boarded a Delta flight headed for Atlanta. Chance and his two men ran up the jet way and onto the plane. The flight attendants were stunned. They looked around the cabin and Chance spotted him in the back of the plane. He reached over another passenger, grabbed Johnny and pulled him out into the aisle.

After he read him his rights, he handcuffed him and took him off the plane and into a waiting car. The crew and airline personnel calmed everyone down and the plane taxied and got ready for takeoff as if nothing had happened. Chance took Johnny into the Davidson Correction Center in downtown Nashville and had him booked. He gave his statement and headed back to the concert site.

No one knew anything about what had just happened. Because of Chance, the crowd saw an outstanding show and enjoyed every minute of it. It could have turned out very differently.

Meanwhile a public defender was being appointed for Johnny. He tried to call Justin with his one phone call but Justin had his phone turned off.

Johnny was booked and held in lockup overnight. He was facing some very serious felony charges.

Chance finally showed up back at the concert site and told me, Justin and Marty he needed to talk to us. Marty kept the lights off but opened up The Hummingbird. It was about 10 pm and most of the crowd had left.

As Chance explained the events of the last couple hours, I started to cry. I knew what a close call this was and that we all could have been killed. Marty called Chance a hero. Chance insisted he was only doing his job and didn't want word of this getting out into the media. Everyone promised to keep it quiet. But you know how things always come out. He didn't want this to affect the rest of the concert series. Justin was thoroughly disgusted with his father and said he could rot in jail.

Chapter 67

Constructing a bomb with intent to kill or inflict bodily harm is a Class 1 Felony in Tennessee and carries a ten-year federal sentence. There are additional explosive charges as well. When Justin saw his father he asked him what the hell he was thinking. There was no way he would be able to weasel his way out of this. Johnny was in some kind of denial, enough so that his lawyer thought he might be able to plead temporary insanity.

Justin said, "Good luck with that. You don't have a prayer. There is so much evidence you're as good as convicted."

I refused to see him. Chance didn't want me anywhere near the jail anyway.

Justin came back to the ranch where Emily was waiting for him. He was so pissed off he could hardly talk. Emily figured it was best to just leave him alone.

It wasn't long before word of this almost disaster started to trickle out. Rumors were flying and Marty was wondering if Chance should just make a statement to say the suspect is in jail and everyone is safe. Chance said he'd talk to his boss, the attorney general, about it. Marty also thought it would be a good idea if I stood with him as Miss Rodeo Tennessee.

"People respect you Becky. They don't know Chance from Adam. No pun intended."

The attorney general agreed that there should be a statement to reassure the public all was well. The news media was alerted and Chance would speak tomorrow morning. I was expected to appear with him.

Chance had his men sweep the grounds one more time and we all piled in the monster truck to go home. I didn't realize how tired I was. With all the excitement, I had forgotten to eat. We stopped at the diner and got some food. Emily was with us because Justin was at the jail with his father. The realization of what Johnny did was just starting to hit me. He must have gone off his rocker or something.

Cassidy didn't know about what happened and we didn't tell her. She didn't have school for a couple days so hopefully things would die down before she went back to school. We didn't want her classmates talking about what happened.

When we finally got home, I just wanted to go to bed. I was so proud of Chance. He was exhausted too and we had to be up early for the news conference. We all laid down and fell asleep with our clothes on. Cassidy thought this was great fun.

The news conference was at 10 am the next morning. I didn't wear my rodeo clothes because a navy blue suit seemed more appropriate. I did wear my tiara though. Chance wore a black suit. That was a first. The attorney general introduced Chance and thanked him for his quick thinking and his calm professional demeanor in the face of an impending tragedy.

Chance repeated that he was only doing his job and just happened to be in the right place at the right time. He said the perpetrator had been arrested and the public was in no further danger. He introduced me as Miss Rodeo Tennessee when it was my turn to speak. A couple people actually clapped.

I said that I was thankful no one was hurt and I hoped everyone would come to the remaining concerts. There was no danger. I thanked those that came the night before and said our first concert was a huge success. Chance hugged me and we all shook hands. It was over.

It took a couple days to recover from all the excitement. Justin was at Johnny's arraignment the next day. The judge refused to grant him bail and kept him in jail until his trial and sentencing in a month. It would not be a jury trial. His fate would lie with one judge.

Emily couldn't understand how Johnny could do such a thing. She didn't think Justin would ever forgive him. She tried to talk to me about it but it was difficult because I didn't have any sympathy for Johnny. I just needed the security of Chance being close by right now.

Chance had begun to talk about getting married again. This time I was more open to the idea and told him I'd think about it. There was no way I could love him more than I already did. I pictured an outdoor wedding in one of the big pastures with all our friends. Marty would give me away and Emily of course would be my maid of honor. Chance's dad would be the best man. I could picture Cassidy all excited as the flower girl dropping rose petals from a basket as she walked by. My dogs would be close by too. Yes, I was definitely thinking about it.

The remaining four concerts went off without a hitch. They were all sold out and there were people standing as far as the eye could see. As promised, twenty percent of the proceeds went to charity. I couldn't think of a better way to spend the money Danny left me. Marty and I both agreed we should do this every year.

The judge sentenced Johnny to ten years in prison. If anyone had been hurt, there would have been a much longer sentence. For now he would be incarcerated at the Davidson Correctional facility in Nashville, but the judge could always change his mind and send him to a federal prison.

Justin was having a hard time with this and Emily was trying to help him by reminding him his career was just beginning and that's where his attention should be. She would stand by him no matter what.

Emily was shocked Johnny was sentenced so harshly.

I just shrugged and said "Karma's a bitch, isn't it?"

"You loved him once," she reminded me.

"Don't remind me," I answered. "He got what he deserved. Think about it. He could have killed a lot of people including us."

Chapter 68

After the concerts were over, Chance and I took Cassidy and we drove up to the Margarita Island Hotel in Pigeon Forge for a couple days. There was so much for a child to do there and we loved seeing her so happy. After she was asleep, Chance and I talked about our future together and we both decided to get married as soon as the wedding could be planned. I promised him Emily and Julie would get right on it. We had to decide where to live and I asked him if he would like to live in a log cabin. He said this had always been a dream of his and I agreed, for it was mine too. So our home would be in the works soon. There was a perfect spot of about two cleared acres near one of the pastures. Life was good and we knew we were blessed. I could feel the love that Chance and I shared as we prepared to become husband and wife.

There was only one more loose end. Chance made reservations to fly to Upstate New York to file sole custody papers for Cassidy. He had all the medical files on Carrie's condition faxed over to his attorney. He was told the waiting period would be three months. If nothing changed, he would have sole custody of his daughter. He wanted to be sure I was on board with this.

"Absolutely," I told him. "You know how much I love this little girl."

It was time to go shopping! Luckily there was a bridal shop in Nashville. Emily and Julie came along to help. Right off the bat, we found the perfect dress! Long, strapless, white satin with a pretty bow in the back. Plain but gorgeous.

Emily and Julie thought they might as well pick out dresses as long as they were there. They chose stunning bridesmaid short dresses in different colors, Emily in green and Julie in coral. The dresses had short sleeves and an off-the-shoulder neckline. Very pretty.

I called Chance and had him bring Cassidy over so we could pick out a dress for her too.

We put our dresses in a fitting room so Chance wouldn't see them. Cassidy bounded into the store, she was so excited. We found her a beautiful satin sleeveless pink and white dress with a big bow in the front. She loved it. All of us would wear white sandals and have flowers in our hair except me. Emily talked me into wearing a short veil. We left the dresses there for alterations and Chance took us all out to lunch. Nobody asked what he would wear but I told him no jeans!

One of Chance's friends was a photographer on the side so that little detail was taken care of.

Marty knew the minister at the white church up the road and asked him if he would officiate at our wedding. He said he'd be delighted.

Justin and Ryan would serve as ushers and Chance's dad would be the best man. Chance decided he should wear a suit if I was wearing a long dress. He and the boys chose a light colored two-piece suit with a vest and long sleeve shirts. I couldn't wait to see how nice they looked.

It was probably a good idea that the wedding was in the late afternoon. That way Chance and I could leave the reception and catch the last flight to Atlanta on the way to Hilton Head for our honeymoon.

There was one thing we decided right away. Invitations would be by word of mouth. Less formal that way. It will be a small wedding, less than 50 people.

Marty and Dixie had their clothes all picked out and we hadn't even set a date yet! Marty said he'd be honored to give me away. Dixie said she'd take care of the flowers. My bouquet would be all daisies and roses in different colors. There would be arrangements of daisies placed all over the wedding site. Cassidy would carry rose petals in a long-handled basket that she would throw as she walked along. She really wanted to throw confetti too and I said I'd think about it. We needed two or three people to walk my dogs down the aisle. How cute would that be? Now if we could just keep the day sunny and bright! I needed to come up with an idea for favors for the guests. I had seen mini western saddles on a cord in a catalog. So when the time came, every guest would have a mini saddle near their dinner plate with "Becky and Chance" and the date embossed on the front of the saddle.

There was a pretty patch of woods with some clear land over near the bunkhouse with room for about 50 chairs. This would be a perfect spot for the wedding. Dixie wanted to have a tent set up in case there was bad weather.

We moved on to the reception. My band said they would be honored to play the music. Dixie would have it catered like she always does when there's a big party. I was excited to see what menu she would come up with. We would use one of the pastures and relocate some of the horses for the day. She would order the wedding cake as soon as we had a date. She promised it would have a cowboy, cowgirl and horse on the top. I couldn't wait to see it!

Everything was coming together. We would have to get a marriage license at the county clerk's office the day before the wedding. It was looking like the wedding could be in two weeks. I asked Chance if he was sure he wanted to marry me. He thought I was joking. He said it can't be soon enough for him. I felt the same way. So we scheduled the wedding two weeks from that Saturday. 16 days! Mrs. Adam Mason. It sounded strange. I would keep my maiden name professionally. We spread the word to everyone involved. Dixie said she'd make up the menu and call the caterers. The flowers would be ordered a day before. Everything would be perfect as long as it didn't rain. Chance told me that's why they make umbrellas.

Dixie showed me the note for the menu.

Menu for wedding reception
Southern shrimp and grits
Fried chicken and biscuit sliders
Chicken and waffles
Biscuits and beans   Fruit tarts
Lemonade and tea cocktails
Peach, blueberry and apple pies
WEDDING CAKE - Vanilla with Chocolate frosting

We all sat back and took some time to think about all this. I remembered I had to order Chance a gift and get presents for Emily, Julie and Cassidy. I had chosen heart necklaces for the girls. I was going to have a money clip engraved for Chance. Meanwhile Chance was preparing to fly to New York to finalize the adoption papers for Cassidy.

Chapter 69

The days seemed to zoom by and before I knew it, the tables were being moved and the chairs were being set up. The weather forecast was excellent, sunny and dry. We didn't need the tent after all. There would be white bows all along the procession route on both sides of the aisles. We had ordered the rings from the local jewelry store and picked them up a few days earlier. We both got simple gold bands. Chance's was wide and very masculine. We decided to go the traditional way with the vows as long as we had a minister.

We had a final fitting for the dresses and brought them home. I hid mine in the main house so Chance wouldn't see it. I told him he had to stay at his parent's the night before the wedding. He didn't like that. The wedding was at 4 pm so he wasn't allowed anywhere around till close to that time. I would get dressed in the main house. Julie was in charge of making sure Cassidy was ready and had her flower petals and basket. I told her she could throw a couple hands of confetti if she wanted to.

We decided that Ryan and Justin would bring the dogs down the aisle right after Cassidy and hand them off to Dixie. Then they would take their places next to Chance. Next would come Julie, Emily and me on Marty's arm. Kelsey hooked up a phone to some speakers to play "Here Comes the

Bride." As a surprise, after the wedding Ryan would go get Skipper who would be all decked out in his show gear, and bring him to me.

Everything was planned and rechecked and on schedule. I wanted to enjoy the moment and not be anxious. I had a hair appointment in the morning and would do my own makeup. There was enough back up around in case anything unforeseen happened. HOORAY! It was going to be a sunny, perfect day.

I woke up by myself because Chance and Cassidy were at his mom's. My wedding day! I just lay there for a minute and soaked it all in. Becky Mason. It would take some getting used to.

Emily was banging around in the kitchen making coffee. She wanted to see me before she went to work. I got up and hugged my best friend. She told me to take it easy and not let my nerves get the best of me. She said she'd see me after lunch.

"Remember Becky, it's a beautiful day and everything will be just perfect. All that matters is that you and Chance will be together."

I took a shower and walked up to the main house to have coffee with Marty and Dixie. My parents were on my mind. I missed them so much, especially on this special day. The sadness that I felt went away when I saw those two smiling faces. I loved them both.

Dixie was cooking up a storm even though it was early. The caterers would bring the rest of the food that afternoon. Marty gave me a big hug and again told me what a good man Chance was. It was nice that we would all be one happy family. I told Dixie that we were going to have traditional vows but in addition we had chosen a short vow to say to each other.

Chapter 70

All of a sudden there were people everywhere setting up chairs and tables and placing the flowers around that had just arrived. Julie was busy as a bee taking care of last minute details. I headed out the door to go into town to have my hair straightened and highlighted. When I got back it would be time to start getting ready. Julie told me not to worry about anything; she had everything under control.

I loved the way my hair looked when it was first done. It usually only lasts one day so that's why I had to go to the salon right before the wedding.

When I got back to the ranch, there was so much going on! Julie had gone to get Cassidy. She ran to me and told me how happy she was that I was going to be her stepmother. This brought tears to my eyes. I loved her so much.

I don't know how but everything came together. I was dressed and ready to walk the pathway five minutes before the hour. The minister was ready and the guests had arrived and were seated. Kelsey had the "Here Comes the Bride" song ready to go. I peeked out the window and saw how handsome the men looked in their suits. Chance took my breath away. I saw Ryan and Justin with my dogs that had fancy collars on. Wow,

I took some deep breaths and was ready when Marty said, "It's time."

Watching out the window, I could see Cassidy walking, tossing her rose petals. I knew the photographer was shooting a video of her. Next came my shelties who somehow knew they were supposed to walk and not play. I stepped outside in time to see Julie who was breathtaking in her coral dress. There was a little space and then Emily, looking gorgeous in green, smiled and walked slowly toward the men who were waiting for me.

Marty said, "smile" and off we went. The music came on and everyone stood. My heart caught in my chest as I locked eyes with Chance. I was filled with emotion but there was no way I was going to cry. Marty kissed me and handed me over to Chance who was grinning from ear to ear. He told me I looked absolutely beautiful. Dixie had my dogs off to the side. They were watching intently and sitting quietly. I hoped Justin remembered the rings.

The ceremony started and everyone sat down. The minister welcomed everyone and said a short prayer. He asked if we were ready to take our vows. We nodded and repeated the traditional vows after him. He knew we had a short vow ready for each other and told us we could recite it next.

Chance went first. "*The first time I saw you my heart whispered 'she's the one.' My heart was so right. You're my special love.*"

Then it was my turn. "*I've always dreamed of marrying a guy like you, and today, I get to marry the man of my dreams. I'll love you forever.*"

The rings were next. Justin didn't forget! We placed the rings on each other's fingers, smiled and recited, "With this ring I thee wed."

199

The judge pronounced us man and wife and told Chance he could kiss his bride. He lifted me off my feet and kissed me. I could feel tears of joy running down my face. Everyone clapped and my dogs barked. Cassidy ran to her father who picked her up and carried her back up the aisle with us.

I saw Ryan standing at the edge of the chairs with Skipper all decked out in his show garb. That was an awesome surprise and it was like the icing on the cake. Chance lifted Cassidy onto Skipper's saddle and we all walked toward the reception area. We started greeting guests and a receiving line formed right there. Even Skipper was in the receiving line! I thought my heart was going to burst, I was so happy. Chance had his arm around me and I hoped it would stay there forever.

"Mr. and Mrs. Adam Mason," Chance kept saying, "You're my wife. I can't believe you're finally my wife." I couldn't believe it either.

There was enough food to feed an army and Dixie outdid herself again. Everything was absolutely delicious. My band got going and they played their hearts out. Nobody asked me to sing, thank goodness. Everyone had a wonderful time clapping and singing with the music. I made a point to talk to every single person that was there so I could thank them for coming.

The cake was brought out and our pictures were taken as we cut into it and fed each other the first piece. That was pretty funny with chocolate frosting everywhere. The catering staff distributed the cake to everyone else and just like that, it was time to throw the bouquet. I didn't look before I threw it and heaved it backwards. Yup, you guessed it, Emily grabbed it. Good for her. I couldn't wait to see the pictures. Chance wasn't keen on the garter thing so we skipped it. There was a table off to the side for wedding gifts. Emily said she'd take good care of them until we got back.

Chapter 71

It was time to leave and catch our flight to Atlanta. Julie got my suitcase and put it in Justin's truck. He put a "Just Married" banner on the rear bumper with cans hanging off making all kinds of noise. I kissed Julie and Emily goodbye and waved to everyone. Cassidy wanted one last hug. I promised her we'd bring her something special. Marty came to the truck to hug me and tell us to have a great honeymoon.

We got to the airport right on time and when we boarded the flight we realized that Chance's dad had us bumped up to first class with free champagne. That was so thoughtful! We had decided to exchange our gifts on the plane. It was like Christmas. Chance gave me a beautiful heart necklace with small diamonds. I absolutely loved it. The money clip I had engraved for him was a hit too. I had his initials put on the front and "I will love you always" engraved on the back.

We made our connection in Atlanta and within an hour we were sitting on the deck of the beautiful house in Hilton Head looking out over the calm, serene ocean. Dusk had just settled in. For a split second I thought of Johnny and the memories of our romance. The memories meant nothing now and seemed like they never happened. Chance was my destiny, my true love, my husband. I adored him. Those pesky whispers and goosebumps were long gone, replaced by a feeling of utter and calming peace.

It was a clear beautiful night filled with stars and an airplane or two. As we watched the heavens, two shooting stars seemed to come out of nowhere and pause right over us.

"Look Chance," I said to my new husband, "I bet that's my momma and daddy looking down at us."

Chance squeezed my hand and kissed me. He said he believed this too and was so happy they approved.

I thought back to when I was a child, talking with my mother about how I would grow up one day and find a wonderful man like my daddy to marry and build a life with. I would wear a long white dress at my wedding and look like a princess. He would be a kind and gentle man and so handsome it would take my breath away. As we continued to watch the sky, two more shooting stars came towards us from the other direction. We stared in awe as they also paused and went right over us again.

I knew in my heart that my parents were giving us their blessing. I'm sure my momma fixed fate so I would live at The Hummingbird Ranch and meet Chance. She knew beyond a shadow of a doubt that I had finally found my dream.

THE END

Retired after many years of working and traveling for the airlines, author Joanne Patterson now spends her time with her three shelties and relaxing with her friends and family. She also enjoys writing and her first romance novel, "Rebecca Steele Chasing a Dream" was published in 2017. This manuscript, based on a true story, sat forgotten in a closet for over 40 years.

Although she has traveled to many places in her life, she prefers living in upstate New York USA where she enjoys the change of seasons and the beautiful countryside. Joanne keeps in touch with family and people she has met over the years on social media. Feel free to contact her directly at
www.facebook.com/authorjoannepatterson

If you enjoyed reading this book, please consider leaving a review for us on Amazon. Thank you!
If you haven't read Book 1, you can find Becky Chasing Her Dream HERE !